Murder Under A Silver Moon

A Mona Moon Mystery
Book Four

Abigail Keam

Worker Bee Press

Special thanks to Melanie Murphy and Liz Hobson.

ISBN 978 17329743 6 4
6 19 2020

Published in the USA by

Worker Bee Press
P.O. Box 485
Nicholasville, KY 40340

1

Every Thursday at four o'clock, Mona Moon held a public tea at Moon Manor, where seven people were allowed to attend. Anyone, from a lowly stable hand to scions of industry, could come provided they made a reservation first with Miss Moon's new social secretary.

Precisely at four, Samuel opened the massive front doors to Moon Manor and escorted a small knot of people into the foyer where the downstairs maid gathered their hats, coats, and gloves before whisking them away to a hidden closet.

The four guests were then greeted by a young woman named Dotty who was wearing a navy polka-dotted dress. "Hello, I'm Miss Dotty, Miss Moon's social secretary. Y'all spoke to me on the phone. Miss Moon will be a few minutes late and begs me to entertain you until she can join us. I would like to ask that you do not attempt to hug Miss Moon nor shake hands with her. Do not attempt to pass food to her." Dotty gave a quick, little smile. "I'm afraid this is not a request. It is a matter of security protocol. I'm sure you understand."

The guests quickly stole glances at each other. They had never heard of such things. Security protocols?

Dotty said, "Please follow me, lady and gentlemen."

Throwing open the double doors to the formal parlor where a fire was lit, Dotty invited the group to partake of the tea sandwiches, tarts, sliced angel food cake, éclairs, and scones along with clotted cream and jams carefully arranged on a buffet table. She poured tea from an antique silver tea service into Royal Doulton porcelain teacups and chatted amiably with the guests, answering their questions about Moon Manor and Mooncrest Farm.

Little did they know at that moment Mona was finishing her own tea upstairs in her bedroom suite with Violet, her maid. She didn't like strangers watching her eat, so Mona had her tea early and went down after her private repast. This gave her guests time to relax somewhat before meeting one of the richest women in the world.

Mona asked, "How do I look?"

Violet perused Mona's black and beige dress which highlighted Mona's platinum hair. "A bit more lipstick, Miss Mona. Your lips look a bit drab."

"Are my seams straight?" Mona asked, looking at her stockings backward into a full length mirror.

"Let me," Violet said as she bent over and pulled a seam straight on Mona's silk hose. "There, that's better."

"I'll be glad when they invent a stocking with no seams." Mona dabbed some red lipstick on and then blotted her lips with a handkerchief. Mona said grinning, "I don't want to look too much like a Jezebel."

"You look fine, Miss."

"How many are down there?"

"Four."

"That's not too bad. What do they want?"

"Pastor Harrod needs a new roof on his

church. He's here to ask if you will donate the money."

"Have I met Pastor Harrod before?"

"Yes, he supported our charity when Babe Ruth came."

"Anything off about him?"

"What do you mean?" Violet asked.

"Does he belong to the Ku Klux Klan? Longing for the days of slave labor? Beat his wife?"

Violet chortled, "Oh no, Miss Mona. He's a sincere, God-fearing man. I've never heard his name associated with anything that smacked of violence or corruption, but he is very old fashioned. He believes in the literal interpretation of the Bible and doesn't believe women should work outside the home."

Mona rolled her eyes.

Seeing Mona bristle at her last statement, Violet said, "His church does a lot for the destitute and is known for helping folks learn to read and write. Jetta based her teaching program on his." When Violet saw Mona recoil at the mention of her former social secretary, Jetta, she hastily apologized. "Sorry, Miss Mona. I didn't mean to bring up Jetta's name. I wasn't thinking."

Jetta was discovered feeding sensitive information to Melanie Moon, Mona's aunt, so Mona gave her the heave-ho. Everyone who worked at Moon Manor had felt betrayed, but Mona was especially devastated.

"I shouldn't be so sensitive. Not your fault. Who else is here asking for money?"

"None that I'm aware. There is a Mr. and Mrs. Kendrick."

"What do they want?"

"They want to introduce themselves and welcome you to Lexington."

"Hmm. Anyone else?"

"A Dr. Rupert Hunt."

"And?"

"He's an assistant professor of history at the University of Kentucky."

Mona smiled. "Finally, someone with whom I can converse." She gave one last glance in the mirror. "Let's get this over with, shall we?"

Violet opened the bedroom door and then locked it behind her before following Mona and Chloe, Mona's pet Standard Poodle, down the grand staircase. It was Mona's policy that her suite should always be locked. Only she and

Violet had a key. That way Mona knew no one could tamper with her things.

Mona had learned the hard way that being rich was also dangerous. Several attempts had been made on her life since she inherited a fortune from her late uncle—Manfred Michael Moon. Also, there had been a rash of high-profile kidnappings, including Charles Lindbergh's baby, which ended in the baby's death, so stringent protocols were put into place. Mona chafed under the new guidelines, but obeyed them. She learned long ago evil walked the earth alongside saints, and sometimes it was hard to discern the difference between the two. Better to be safe than sorry.

Chloe loped into the parlor first while Mona waited in the foyer listening. If there were oohs and ahhs upon seeing Chloe, Mona knew her guests were friendly and dog lovers. A good thing in Mona's eyes. If there were cries of dismay and frantic shooing away, Mona would be less inclined to accommodate her guests with their requests. It was one of Mona's prejudices. She disliked people who disliked animals, especially *her* dog.

Chloe was greeted enthusiastically, which made Mona smile. She took a deep breath, plastered a smile on her face, and strode into the parlor. "Hello."

The men stood immediately as Mona personally greeted each one. "Pastor Harrod, nice to see you again."

"I'm flattered that you remember me."

"How could I forget?"

Pastor Harrod blushed and his hands, dotted with brown-age spots trembled a bit.

Mona turned to the middle-aged couple with their tweed jackets and sensible shoes. They looked like the outdoorsy types. "Mr. and Mrs. Kendrick, I understand."

Mr. Kendrick extended his hand, forgetting Dotty's instructions. His wife tugged on his jacket. Embarrassed, Mr. Kendrick stuck his hand away in his pants pocket, not knowing what else to do.

Mona pretended not to notice. "So nice to meet the both of you. I don't think we've met before, have we?"

Mrs. Kendrick spoke up. "We have not, indeed. Mr. Kendrick has been under the weather this past year. We even missed Babe Ruth coming to town. I hear the event was a smashing success."

"I was sorrowful about that. I love baseball and keep up with all the statistics," Mr. Kendrick added.

"I'm sorry to hear about your poor health, Mr. Kendrick. Please sit down. Gentlemen, all of you, please sit."

The men sat and replaced their napkins upon their laps.

Dotty offered Mona a cup of tea, which she accepted before settling into a chair.

"I hope you are feeling better, Mr. Kendrick," Mona said.

"I am, Miss Moon. Thank you."

Mrs. Kendrick piped up, "Moon Manor is beautiful."

"Thank you, Mrs. Kendrick. After the fire last year, I wasn't sure if we could get the manor back to its original state, but I think our local craftsmen did a wonderful job." Mona turned to the youngest member of the group. "You are Doctor Rupert Hunt."

"Yes, Miss. Thank you for letting me come.

Oh, and please don't feel you need to address me by my honorific."

"I'm an academic myself. You should be proud of the title 'doctor.'"

"Thank you."

"I've not been able to become acquainted with everyone in the community, so this is my small way of meeting people. Dr. Hunt, I understand that you are an assistant professor of history at the University of Kentucky."

Dr. Hunt placed his teacup on the side table and scooted forward on his chair. "Yes, Miss. I am a most fortunate man to receive the post. I hope to make tenure soon."

Mona asked, "What is your field of expertise?"

"I focus on North America between 1600 to 1850, especially this area."

Mona said, "I see. I'm very interested in archaeology myself. I made my living by being a cartographer for most of my adulthood."

Dr. Hunt said, "I understand you were in Iraq."

Mona nodded. "Several times. I am fascinated by the peoples of Mesopotamia—the Sumerians and the Babylonians."

"Mesopotamia, the cradle of civilization," Dr. Hunt commented.

Pastor Harrod interjected, "Abraham was born in Ur."

"Was he really?" Mrs. Kendrick said. "I guess I need to read my Bible more often. I thought Abraham was born in Canaan."

"He was promised Canaan by God, but he was born in Ur," Pastor Harrod said.

Mischievously, Mona added, "Yes, Abraham left his father, Terah, in Ur while taking his wife Sarah, who was also his half-sister."

Mrs. Kenrick's eyes grew large. "Goodness. Is that true, Reverend? Was Sarah Abraham's half-sister?"

Pastor Harrod blushed and tugged at his tie. "It's not something we like to address except to say things were different back then. The terms sister, brother, daughter, son are given large latitude in the Bible. I guess to say that we might suspect, but we don't really know."

Mona smiled into her cup of tea.

Wishing to dispel the awkwardness of the moment, Dr. Hunt spoke up, "Pastor Harrod, are you a descendant of James Harrod?"

Pleased that someone had made the connection to his famous ancestor, Pastor Harrod said, "Yes, I'm proud to say that I am a descendant."

Mona said, "I am not up on all my Kentucky history yet, so please fill me in."

"James Harrod established the first permanent settlement in Kentucky called Harrodsburg," Dr. Hunt said, sneaking Chloe a bit of his cucumber tea sandwich.

"I thought Daniel Boone established the first permanent European settlement at Boonesborough," Mona said.

Dr. Hunt shook his head. "Boone tried earlier but failed. However, he did blaze the Wilderness Road through the Cumberland Gap into Kentucky."

"I have never understood what the Cumberland Gap is," Mr. Kendrick said.

Dr. Hunt replied, "It was basically a natural break through the mountains that the Indians used. A footpath, really. Boone made part of it wider and it was called the Wilderness Trail. It opened the door to the West through the Appalachian Mountains. Otherwise, settlers had to come down the Ohio River on flatboats in the spring when the water ran high."

"I am learning so much today," Mrs. Kendrick said, raising a cup to her lips.

Dr. Hunt continued, "I am so pleased to meet you, Pastor Harrod. I have a special interest in your ancestor."

The Pastor asked, "Why is that?"

"I understand James Harrod disappeared off the face of the earth on a hunting trip."

"It truly is a mystery as to what happened to him," Pastor Harrod lamented.

"I'm not familiar with the story," Mona said, suddenly very interested in James Harrod. She leaned forward in her chair. "I love a good mystery. What happened?"

"You explain it, Dr. Hunt," Pastor Harrod encouraged. "You probably can tell the tale better than I."

Dr. Hunt wiped his mouth with the linen napkin and folded it neatly. "Well, if you won't be bored then I shall. It's a story with lots of blood and guts."

Petting Chloe and sneaking her a biscuit, Mona said, "Please do. I like a good yarn with blood and guts."

"Really, Miss Moon," Mrs. Kendrick admonished.

"I'm just teasing, Mrs. Kendrick, but Dr. Hunt does make it sound intriguing," Mona said, keeping her face as that of a sphinx. "Go on, Dr. Hunt. I really am interested." Mona disliked someone correcting her in her own home eating her food, but tried not to show irritation. She had the teas to make friends, not to correct people's social manners.

Obviously, quite pleased with himself, Dr. Hunt said, "James Harrod was an enterprising and capable man. He served in the French and Indian War, founded Harrodsburg, owned more than 20,000 acres of land in Kentucky, and was awarded the rank of colonel in the local militia. He was respected by his community and was elected to the Virginia House of Delegates as Kentucky was part of Virginia at that time. Later on, James served as trustee for Harrodsburg. He was a master frontiersman in every sense of the word—honorable, charitable, outstanding hunting skills, remarkable rifle shot, and fearless in the face of danger."

"Sounds like my kind of man," Dotty remarked.

"Another noteworthy thing about James Harrod is that his brother, Sam, and his father's first wife were killed by the Indians. Even his wife's father, first husband, and their son were killed by them. Her father was scalped, and the son was burned at the stake. Yet, James Harrod was known for not hating Indians."

"He was a man who practiced his faith," Pastor Harrod said. "Love thy neighbor."

"Still, with all the bloodshed on the frontier over land rights, that was an unusual attitude for a white man," Mona said. "I'm impressed, but he was still stealing land from the indigenous people, was he not?"

Pastor Harrod pursed his lips together and refused to comment, even though he felt insulted. He needed a roof for his church and by God, this white haired vixen with her yellow eyes was going to get it for him.

Mrs. Kendrick asked, "What happened to James Harrod?"

Dr. Hunt petted Chloe, who whined wanting to be scratched behind her ears. "In February of 1792, James entered the Kentucky wilderness with Michael Stoner, a friend, and another man named Bridges on an apparent beaver hunting trip. James did not return with them from the trip."

"What happened?" Mona asked.

"That's it. No one knows," Dr. Hunt said. "According to James' wife, Ann, there was bad blood between Bridges and James over land several years back. She warned James not to go with him."

Mr. Kendrick asked, "Was a body ever found?"

"Yes and no," Dr. Hunt replied. "I'll get to that in a moment."

"The feud must have been forgotten if James went on a hunting trip with this fellow," Mrs. Kendrick said.

"Ann didn't think so," Pastor Harrod replied. "According to her statement, she begged James not go to with Bridges, and James must have put some credence in what Ann said because shortly before the trip, he wrote a new will giving everything to his wife and daughter and asked his friend, Stoner, to go with him."

"Ah," Mona said.

Pastor Harrod said, "Some claim that James

decided upon a 'wilderness divorce' and just walked away from his family."

"And leave all that wealth behind? Most men I know wouldn't walk away from their life's work and money regardless of how they felt about the missus," Mona said.

"I don't think so, either," Dr. Hunt concurred. "Many settlers claimed James 'worshipped' his wife. Ann publicly stated she felt Bridges murdered James out of revenge."

"What happened?" Dotty asked. She leaned forward and thought the story was better than any she read in the dime store mystery novels she bought. She thought Dr. Hunt was handsome with his auburn hair, corn blue eyes, and ruddy cheeks. He looked solid in his gray wool suit with his wide shoulders and narrow waist. Dr. Hunt had a jovial aura about him that was infectious.

Dr. Hunt gave Dotty a warm smile. "According to Stoner, the three camped on the Three Forks of the Kentucky River. We call the location Beattyville now. Stoner claimed he was making breakfast when James and Bridges went to check their traps. Suddenly, Bridges rushed back to camp where he said he heard a shot from James's area of the traps. Stoner and Bridges waited but James did not return."

Dotty said, "Doesn't sound good."

Dr. Hunt continued, "Bridges went to look for James and came back saying he saw fresh Indian tracks but no Harrod. Stoner wanted to look for James, but Bridges talked him out of it, and the two return to Harrodsburg."

"The entire story sounds fishy to me," Mona stated.

"In what way?" Pastor Harrod asked.

Mona answered, "I take it that all three men were marksmen and fearless. They would have to be to live in the wilderness, so why is Stoner hanging around the campfire while Bridges is looking for James? He should have been looking as soon as James didn't come back to camp, especially knowing about the past bad blood between Bridges and James. All three of these men were superb trackers. If James was hurt, the two other men could have easily tracked him down."

Pastor Harrod offered an explanation, "Perhaps Stoner was wary of violence from Bridges and feared the man would shoot him as well if he went to look for James."

"I think so, too," Dr. Hunt agreed. "There's another thing which points to murder—when Bridges returned, he sold some furs and silver buttons with the letter H engraved on them. The shopkeeper sent the buttons to Ann Harrod and she identified them as belonging to her husband."

Pastor Harrod interrupted, "But several witnesses said they saw James Harrod months later being held captive by Indians near Detroit."

Mona said, "If I remember my American history, families of rich abductees were usually contacted for a ransom. The Indians would have known who James Harrod was and asked for a trade in either money or a prisoner swap."

"Was a body ever found, Pastor Harrod?" Dotty asked.

"Yes, one, but it was not conclusively identified. James' friends searched for him and found some bones in a cave. The bones were wrapped in sedge grass and apparently had been dragged there. His friends claimed the skeleton was wearing James' shirt with the silver buttons missing."

"See, that proves murder," Mrs. Kendrick

said, looking about for support.

"It doesn't prove anything," Dr. Hunt said. "As far as I know, the friends didn't bring back the bones or the shirt. Do you know, Pastor Harrod?"

"I've never been able to find a record of that body. Could have been an Indian set to eternal rest there."

"So, no one knows if James' friends even found a body, let alone James Harrod's corpse."

"That's right," Pastor Harrod said, reaching for a tea sandwich Dotty offered to him. "Strange tale, indeed."

"But the story doesn't end there," Dr. Hunt alleged. "Ann Harrod claimed the three were really hunting for John Swift's silver mine, and the beaver hunting trip was a cover story."

Mona asked, "Who is John Swift? Are we discussing the writer, John Swift of Gulliver's Travels?"

"No. No." Mr. Kendrick waved his hand in dismissal. "It's an old legend. A wives' tale really. John Swift supposedly discovered a silver mine the Indians used, mined it, and then hid treasure throughout the region."

Pastor Harrod added, "Only to go blind and could never find his treasure again."

Mrs. Kendrick's hand fluttered to her throat. "Oh my, I didn't know that."

Mona laughed. "Sounds very similar to the old Dutchman's Lost Mine story."

Dr. Hunt tugged at his tie, trying to gather his courage. Out of sheer excitement, he jumped up. "That's why I wanted to meet you, Miss Moon. I think John Swift's mine does exist, and James Harrod was murdered trying to find it. There are eyewitness accounts that James Harrod was not in Central Kentucky hunting, but in the mountains looking for the mine. I am planning an expedition to the mountains to search, and I would like you to go with me."

Mona remained motionless until Dotty said, "The hour is up. Pastor Harrod, thank you for coming. We will send you a letter about your proposal for a new roof. Mr. and Mrs. Kendrick, it was a pleasure to meet you."

Mona stood as well. "Yes, it was. You must come again."

Dotty turned to Dr. Hunt, who looked longingly at Mona for an answer. "Dr. Hunt, send us a written proposal, and Miss Moon will look it over."

"I am leaving in a week. I hope you do come, Miss Moon. I'm not a cartographer, and the only one at the university is on sabbatical. I'm afraid I need you."

Dotty stretched out her arm showing the way out. "Mr. Thomas will show you the way out. Thank you again for coming."

Thomas, the butler, opened the doors of the parlor and escorted the guests to the foyer where Samuel and a maid waited with their coats, hats, and gloves. Before showing the guests to the front door, he closed the door to the parlor leaving Mona and Dotty alone.

Dotty filled another plate with some angel cake slices. "I'm starving."

"You're going to ruin your dinner," Mona commented.

Dotty looked at her watch. "Dinner's not for another three hours. I'll be starving by then."

"Quite. I think I'll have some more scones."

"Didn't you have tea in your room?"

Mona grinned, "Yeah, but who could resist these goodies. I'm developing a sweet tooth, I'm afraid."

"Who's got a sweet tooth?" Lord Farley said, striding into the room, wearing riding jodhpurs and black boots. He went over to Mona and kissed her on the cheek.

"You smell like a sweaty horse, Robert," Mona said.

"So sorry," Lord Farley replied, sniffing his shirt. "My horse is tied up out front. We both had a good romp this afternoon."

"Don't apologize. I like the smell of horses."

"So, who's got a sweet tooth?"

Dotty pointed at Mona. "Mona's got one for sure. This is her second tea of the day."

Lord Farley said, "Better be careful, girl. Don't want to get fat."

Mona's eyes flashed. "It always annoys me when men say silly quips like that, especially if they're not exactly matinee idols themselves."

"You said I was handsome."

"That's not the point, Robert. Men want women to be pretty, but do they try to make themselves attractive for women? No, they don't. They don't even think about their looks when it comes to women. The ugliest, ill-groomed man always makes a pitch to the prettiest gal in the room. He can't even conceive that he might be repulsive to her."

"I didn't mean to start a war."

Quickly placing more tarts and cream on her plate, Dotty said, "I'll think I'll take my goodies and leave."

"Oh, don't, Dotty. We fight like this on a daily basis. I always say something wrong," Farley said.

"Yes, stay, Dotty. Tell Lord Farley about our tea guests."

Lord Farley plopped lazily into a chair. "Yes, tell me how bad it was this time. I told you, Mona, not to open your doors to the great unwashed. They'll never appreciate anything you do for them and secretly resent you for your help."

"Robert, please keep your British upper class snobbism out of my parlor. What happened to noblesse oblige?"

Lord Farley held up his hand. "Before you and Dotty attack me further for being uncharitable and unfeeling, I'm not talking about class distinctions. I am referring to human nature. As long as you have something a lot of people want and don't possess, you'll be loathed for it, no matter how many good works you spend your money on."

"What am I supposed to do, Robert? Let people starve in my community when I have so much? There is a Depression going on."

"I'm saying don't expect people to like you for it, Mona."

"Money is like manure, Robert. It should be spread around a little."

Lord Farley picked an apple from an end table and chomped into it. "Who put the bite on Mona today, Dotty?"

"Pastor Harrod wants a new roof for his church."

"Ah, that pompous ass. He bores me to tears."

Mona said, "Actually, I found him quite interesting."

Lord Farley quit munching on his apple. "Really?"

Dotty interjected, "We had a lively discussion about the disappearance of James Harrod who is an ancestor of Pastor Harrod. He was joined by Dr. Rupert Hunt, who was just as knowledgeable."

Lord Farley asked, "Who is James Harrod and why do we care that he disappeared?"

Mona freshened up her tea. "He was one of the original settlers in Kentucky and is thought to have been murdered."

"Is he the pioneer that Harrodsburg is named after?" Farley asked.

"Yes," Dotty answered. "There is a legend that he went missing while searching for a lost silver mine. Dr. Hunt is going to look for it and wants Mona to join him."

Lord Farley gave a raspberry. "Lost silver mine? Where? In South America?"

"Here—in the mountains," Mona said.

"There's no silver in Kentucky."

"We did say it was lost, Robert."

Startled, Lord Farley sat up. "Don't you think with all the coal mines honeycombing Eastern Kentucky someone would have stumbled upon a silver mine by now?"

Mona smiled.

"I don't like that look on your face, Mona. You're not thinking of joining this crackpot expedition?" Farley asked. He looked between Mona and Dotty.

"A lost silver mine and a possible murder of

one of Kentucky's founding fathers—how can I resist?" Mona said, watching Lord Farley's expression as he suddenly stood up. "Where are you going?"

"Home to clean and pack my guns. You don't think I'm going to let you go into the mountains without me, do you?"

"You were not invited to join the expedition, Robert."

Lord Farley grinned, "Righty ho, but going I am, dearest, so don't get your knickers in a twist. I'll be over for dinner tonight, so tell Samuel to set an extra plate."

Mona watched Lawrence Robert Emerton Dagobert Farley stride out of the room. "Dotty, see how easy it is. If you want a man to do something, just act as though you don't. They fall for it every time."

"You want Lord Farley to join you?"

"I don't know this Rupert Hunt but I do trust Lord Farley. He's a good man to have your back." Mona rose and put her plate and teacup on the side table. "I'd better tell Violet to purchase some sturdy boots for me and get all my outdoor clothes ready. Dotty, I'm going silver mine hunting!"

2

Dexter Deatherage was apoplectic. "You can't do this, Mona. It's reckless."

Mona looked down the barrel of a revolver she was cleaning. "But I am."

"As your lawyer, I am advising you this trip places you in grave danger."

"I'm tired of parties, endless meetings, and teas with strangers. I need this trip. I need to get away from all the pomp and circumstance surrounding my life. I need an adventure or at least a vacation."

"And you think Eastern Kentucky is going to be restful?" Dexter pulled the gun out of Mona's hand. "Listen to me. The Appalachian Mountains are a dangerous place. There are few roads and what roads exist are mostly dirt. You have to go on horseback, and you'll be cut off from contact. You could run into a blood feud like the Hatfields and McCoys."

Mona grabbed her gun back. "That feud ended years ago."

"Mona, you are placing yourself in jeopardy for a kidnapping. At least, take some of the Pinkertons with you."

"Lord Farley is accompanying me."

Dexter threw up his hands. "Oh, great. Another prime target for kidnapping. Lord Farley is in line for the throne of England. Why don't you put a bullseye on his back—hey IRA—here's a British royal for the taking?"

Mona gave an irritated sigh. "I hardly think the Irish Republic Army is ensconced in Eastern Kentucky."

"Who do you think those people descended from? The Irish and Scotch-Irish."

"Robert is not British royalty."

"He's a high-ranking noble who only recently lost his royal title."

"His father did, not Robert."

"Quit splitting hairs, Mona. You know what I mean."

"No one will even know who he is. If the mountains are as isolated as you say, the people will never have heard of a Lord Farley, Marquess of Gower, future Duke of Brynelleth, ninth in line to the throne of Great Britain. He is going as Bob Farley."

"I can't help but think this is a huge mistake. What if your Aunt Melanie hears of this? She'll use it to her advantage and create chaos."

"No one knows I'm leaving. Not even my staff. I'll leave a note with Violet and be back before two shakes of a lamb's tail. You can handle things while I'm gone. As far as anyone is concerned, I'll be taking a short holiday. For all I know, this is a hoax and we'll be back in a few days."

Frustrated, Dexter continued, "Look what happened to Mary McElroy in Missouri earlier this year. She was kidnapped taking a bubble bath in her own home and held captive."

"For twenty-nine hours. I hardly call that an event."

"I'm sure it was to Miss McElroy, who was dragged naked from her bubble bath by strange men. I hear she has had a nervous breakdown over this 'non-event.'"

"I didn't mean to sound flippant. I'm sure it was terrifying for her. You forget that my best friend, Lady Alice, was kidnapped only a short time ago."

"And while she was missing, how did you feel, Mona?"

Mona bowed her head. "Awful. Not in control. Beside myself with worry."

"Precisely. Remember the Charles Lindbergh baby? He was killed within the first hours of the kidnapping, and he was taken from his own bedroom—his own bed in a house full of live-in staff, and he still wasn't safe. You'll be out in the middle of nowhere—helpless."

Mona stopped cleaning her guns and looked Dexter squarely in the face. "You must stop this ranting, Dexter. It's unseemly. I know you are acting in my interest, but I can't live like this. It's not a real life being guarded like I was a prize pig at the state fair. I can't go where I please anymore. Even when I take a walk on my own estate, I have a shadow following me. It's downright creepy, not to mention intrusive. Dexter, my dear friend, what I can't get you to understand is that I would rather face danger than live a safe, dull life. I must do this for my peace of mind."

"I can't talk you out of this?"

"No, and I wish you'd quit harping on it."

"When are you leaving?"

"Soon enough."

"When are you coming back?"

"If I'm not back two weeks after I've left, then you have permission to call out the dogs."

"Great," Dexter said, angrily while putting on his hat. "Just great. You can't talk sense to a stubborn woman."

Mona watched him leave the room and heard the front door open and slam shut. She shrugged, figuring Dexter would get over it. She understood Dexter's concern and, in many ways he was correct, but Mona couldn't live her life in a vacuum. She was suffocating under all the restrictions and needed to get away where she could relax and not be on parade. This little expedition was just the ticket.

Oh, Mona doubted they would find the mythical John Swift's silver mine. It didn't matter since she was looking for something other than riches.

Mona was looking for adventure!

3

"Did you remember to lock the door when you sneaked out at six in the morning?" Lord Farley teased, hopping into the truck and pushing Chloe toward Mona.

"Chloe and I had to creep past the guards to get to the barn where we keep the farm vehicles."

"I would beef up my security, Mona. If a woman with white hair and a white dog can get past all those guards, they must be taking a snooze. Even with the moon only a quarter full, they should have spotted you."

"I thought the same myself."

"I told my staff I was going to New York. What did you tell yours?"

"Left a note on Violet's dressing table and told her the same. I'll send a telegram from

Richmond to Dexter letting him know that I'm gone. He'll be the only one who knows of our expedition."

"I don't understand the need for all this secrecy."

"Apparently, there are treasure hunters still looking for the Swift mine, and they would follow us."

Lord Farley harrumphed. "There is no silver mine. This Swift story is one of the most ridiculous tall tales I've ever heard. All geologists say there is no silver in Kentucky."

"If you feel that way, why are you coming?"

"To be alone in the woods with the woman of my dreams."

"Well, you're going to be disappointed. There are going to be others besides Hunt on this trip."

"Tarnation. Why doesn't anything go my way where you are concerned?"

"Tarnation? You *are* picking up the local lingo."

"Woman, shake your tail feathers. Let's get a move on."

Mona laughed as she pressed on the gas pedal and put the truck into first gear. "Yes, sir!"

Both Mona and Farley grimaced as the truck made a racket heading out Farley's driveway. Mona turned right on the country road.

"Where are we going?" Lord Farley asked.

"We are going to meet Rupert at Mary Breckinridge's place in Hyden, Kentucky."

"First name basis with Dr. Hunt, huh? When did that happen?"

"I guess at all the meetings we had concerning this venture, none of which you bothered to attend. You know Rupert is the same age as I am, and we share the same interests. We've become very close." Mona stole a look at Farley.

He reacted impassively. "I figured you would have everything sewn up so why should I attend?"

"Then don't buck me when things don't go your way on this trip." Mona changed gears, and the truck was doing a brisk thirty-five miles per hour.

"What's in the back of the truck?"

"Supplies. Tents. Food. That sort of thing."

Farley pushed Chloe off again. "Get off, Chloe. You're crushing me."

"She wants to look out the window. You're

blocking her view." Mona hit a bump, and everyone in the truck bounced up and hit their heads on the roof.

"There is no view. It's still dark. Let me drive," Farley complained.

"You can later. I might want to take a nap after Richmond."

"So I take it that we are going via London and then cut east over to Hyden."

"It's the most direct route but I think the road to Hyden is going to be a bit rough."

"We'll need to gas up before we hit London."

"We can gas up the truck in Richmond and I brought extra fuel—just in case. It's in the back of the truck."

"Great. I hope no one hits us." Farley cried out, "WATCH OUT! THERE'S A DEER!"

Mona swerved and narrowly missed the frightened doe before straightening out the truck. "We're going to have this problem all the way. I'm keeping a lookout for them."

"You do that. I am going to take a little snooze myself." Farley took off his jacket and rammed it under his head. "Wake me up when we get to Richmond. We should eat when we get there."

Mona said, "Look back behind the seat. There should be a basket with food. It will tide us over until we reach Richmond."

"Better hang on to it. Richmond is only an hour or so away. After Richmond, the largest town will be London. There won't be anywhere to eat in between." Farley lay back and closed his eyes, impervious to the jostling the truck made on the single lane road until Mona pulled out onto US 25, which was the main two-lane highway going south.

Chloe situated herself so that her head and shoulders were resting on Farley's lap. Occasionally her tail wagged until both she and Farley were asleep and snoring.

It had begun to drizzle and then the rain came in earnest—sheets of it. Determined to make good time, Mona kept alert at the wheel but heavy rain slowed her down. Finally, a frustrated Mona pulled into a Pure Oil gas station in Richmond.

A man in a rain slicker came running out.

Mona rolled down her window. "Fill 'er up, please."

"Check the oil and radiator, ma'am?"

"No need." Mona looked over the road to a restaurant. "Mister, that place over there good to eat? I see a lot of truckers stop there."

"Only place in town open for breakfast," the gas jockey said, before turning on the pump.

"That's not much of a recommendation," Mona muttered under her breath.

"What's that," Farley mumbled, stirring awake.

Chloe rose on the seat and shook.

"We're in Richmond and filling up. There's a place open across the street."

"Good. I'm starving."

Mona paid the attendant and drove the truck to the restaurant, parking off to the side. "Stay here, Chloe and guard the truck. I'll bring you something to eat." She jumped down and inspected the tires before following Farley into the eatery.

Everyone in the joint gave Farley and Mona the once over as they entered, but soon went back to talking amongst themselves. The only seats available were at the counter. Mona and Farley slid onto the round wooden seats.

A waitress chewing gum came over to them

and slapped some menus down in front of them. "What can I do you for?"

"Black coffee, please. No cream for both of us," Mona said.

The waitress shuffled off.

Farley opened his menu. "I'm going to get some eggs sunny-side up and bacon and some flapjacks."

Lowering her voice, Mona said, "You are not going to order any such thing. Restaurants such as these are notorious for giving one the trots. No one inspects them. I've heard of a traveling salesman named Duncan Hines, who has a list of good restaurants to eat around the country. I hear he's going to publish his list into a booklet."

"Well, I'm hungry now. I can't wait for this Duncan Hines."

"Shush. I'll order for you. Your English accent is a dead giveaway."

The waitress came back with two steaming cups of hot coffee. Taking a pencil out of her brown wavy hair, she asked, "Ready?"

Mona answered, "Yes, we'll both have scrambled eggs, country ham, and toast. I also want an extra helping of ham please."

"Red-eye gravy with that?"

"Yes, please."

While writing the order down, the waitress glanced at Mona's and Farley's hands. Seeing that Mona was wearing a wedding band, she became friendlier. Immoral women were known to travel with truck drivers. The owner of the restaurant didn't like them coming into his place. They always caused trouble with the customers. She took in Mona's simple blue printed feed sack dress, cardigan sweater, ankle socks, and sturdy shoes. A cotton scarf covered most of Mona's hair but the waitress was startled at Mona's white hair peeping out from the scarf and her amber eyes.

Noticing the waitress' surprised look, Mona said, thumbing at Farley, "I saw a Jean Harlow movie and wanted to spice up our marriage but he hates it. Gotta keep my hair covered until the dye grows out."

The waitress shot a look at Farley. "You can never please them. Never. My old man says I'm getting fat, but I'm the same weight I was when I married him. I don't know what gets into men. They just like to complain." She turned in their orders and rang customers up on the cash register before pouring coffee for others who waved at her. She stood and chatted with several of the men, hoping to inspire them to leave a good tip.

A bell rang in the window leading to the kitchen.

"Your order is up," she called over to Mona and Farley.

"That was quick," Mona said.

"Doesn't take long to scramble some eggs," Farley grumbled.

The waitress got their orders and topped their coffee before shuffling over to a new customer.

Farley looked glumly at his scrambled eggs. "I really wanted sunny-side up. These eggs look overcooked."

"Eat. This way everything is heated through, and all the germs are killed. The yolks in sunny-side eggs may harbor dangerous bacteria, so it's best to eat scrambled. Country ham is salt cured, so you can eat it unheated and it couldn't hurt you."

Farley shook salt and pepper on his eggs and cut into his country ham. Taking a bite, he said, "Not bad. Not bad at all, I must say. This gravy is most curious."

"It's made from the drippings of fried country ham mixed with black coffee."

Farley took a few more bites before gesturing at Mona's left hand. "What's with the wedding band?"

"It's best that I travel as a married woman. You are to pose as my husband."

"Thanks for letting me in on the plan." He drank some coffee and motioned to the waitress for more. "You know we can make that really happen. Give me a date and I'll set it up. Maybe we can find a justice of the peace on this trip. You've already got the ring."

"I told you I'm not ready to get married."

"Can we at least tell people we are engaged?"

"But we're not."

"You said yes."

"I did not."

"Yes, you did, Mona. Keep this up and you will be too old to marry. The bloom on the rose won't last forever, and I won't want you when you're fat and wrinkled."

"Charming." Mona stuck her tongue out at Farley who made a face at her.

They finished their meal and as Farley paid

the bill, Mona went in search of a bathroom. She found an old-fashioned outhouse in the back. Gritting her teeth, she did her business and then went in search of a whiskey bottle she had put in the back of the truck.

"Why are you pouring good whiskey on your hands, Mona?" Farley asked, feeding Chloe country ham.

"You would too if you used their bathroom."

"You'll smell like a distillery."

"I'll douse my hands with water," she replied, pulling out a large jug of spring water. She poured water over her hands and then poured water in a bowl for Chloe. "Come girl. Drink up and then do your business. We gotta go."

Farley went in search of the bathroom as several men came out of the restaurant and upon seeing Chloe, pointed and laughed.

"Pay them no mind, Chloe," Mona said.

"Give me some of that," Farley said, hurrying back and thrusting out his hands. "I'm about to throw up. It stank so badly in there."

Mona poured it over Farley's hands as he washed with the golden liquid. Then she poured water on them.

Farley sniffed. "We both stink like a distillery now."

"The smell will evaporate. Let's get going."

"Wait a minute." Farley ran back into the restaurant and after several minutes came out with several little green bottles of Coca-Cola and a paper sack with four pieces of pecan pie wrapped in wax paper. "The bottles are cold," he said cheerfully as he picked Chloe up and put her in the front seat of the truck before climbing into the driver's seat.

"Oh, you spoke. You shouldn't have done that, Robert."

"Naw, I grunted as to what I wanted and pointed. Quit being such a worry wart." Farley opened his hand. "Look. I got a hobo nickel back as change."

Mona reached up and picked the nickel from his hand, inspecting the carved nickel. Hobos and tramps sometimes carved the figure on the buffalo nickel into a different configuration and put them back into circulation. "Can I keep this? I collect them."

"Be my guest." Farley looked in the side mirrors. "Let's get moving. Get in, milady. Your chariot awaits."

Mona went around to the other side of the truck and climbed in the passenger side. Opening a Coke, she gratefully drank. "The carbonation always settles my stomach."

"Mine too," Farley said as they headed out on US 25.

Mona took a nap and awoke as Farley pulled into another gas station in London. She rolled down her window. The rain had stopped and the mountain air smelled wonderfully fresh. Mona took a deep breath. "Magnificent," she muttered to Chloe. "Smells differently from home."

Chloe sniffed and then sneezed.

While Farley ordered gas from the gas jockey and checked the tires, Mona let Chloe out for a bathroom break and put her back in the truck after seeing other customers take note of Chloe. She used the gas station's bathroom, grateful for its modern plumbing and toilet paper. After washing her hands, she hurried back to the truck and broke out the last piece of pecan pie, giving some to Chloe before eating the rest herself. Hungry, she pulled the picnic basket out from the back of the truck.

Farley found her eating a roast beef sandwich

sitting at a picnic table the gas station owner had put underneath some trees. Other customers were eating their packed lunches as well at other tables as it had stopped raining. "Started without me?"

"The way you gobble up food, I had to. If I didn't know how old you are, I'd swear you're still growing."

"I'll let Chloe out."

"No, don't. Eat first," Mona said. "I let her out as soon as we got here, and she got too much attention. Apparently, most folks around here have never seen a Standard Poodle."

"That would make sense. You have to have a dog that will pay for its keep. I told you not to bring her."

"She is a working breed. I'll remind you that poodles are hunting and retrieving dogs. That's why they were bred."

"And I'll remind you that poodles are now only kept by wealthy women as companions. Poodles haven't been used as hunting dogs for fifty years now."

"Well, it's done now. I couldn't leave her. She would have barked her head off if I had left her locked up in my bedroom. I'll let her out when these folks leave, but let's put her on a leash. If she runs off chasing a squirrel, we don't have the time to find her in this rough terrain." Mona sighed. "Let's not argue. Here. Have a sandwich."

Grabbing a sandwich, Farley looked around. "We're deep in the mountains now. Where do we go from here?"

"We'll turn east on Route 80. We lost good time due to the rain, but it shouldn't be too much longer."

"The truck is rough riding on these windy, curvy roads," Farley said, stretching his back.

"It's only going to get more curvy from here on out."

"Great."

"Do you think we'll ever build roads like the autobahn in Germany?"

"We would be smart to do so," Farley said. "Quick way to move troops, and it would be a pleasure to drive on a straight concrete road. Whatever you might say about the Germans, they are a clever and industrious people."

"Do you think Hitler is building the autobahn to move troops?"

"Who knows? I hope Ramsay MacDonald is keeping a close eye on him. Hitler's rhetoric bothers me greatly, and his hatred toward minority groups, especially the Jews, is bothersome. Somehow I don't think the man is just spouting propaganda. Either way, he's got everyone in Germany worked up. It's bizarre how many Germans think he's the second coming of Christ."

"Maybe Hitler's full of hot air and will calm down now that he's in power."

Farley threw wax paper into the trash bin. "Let's hope so." He looked at the sun. "After midday. We better get a move on if we hope to make the Frontier Nursing Service by this evening."

"Look, everyone has gone. Let's take one last potty break. Get some more Cokes, will ya, Robert?"

"Sure, but hurry. The sky is dark. It seems like the rain is following us. You go on. I'll take Chloe for a short walk while you freshen up."

Mona ran to the bathroom where she combed her hair and put on some lipstick after washing her face. She felt human again. When she came out, Farley and Chloe were already in the truck waiting.

She climbed up into the driver's seat and put the truck into its hurly-burly, bouncy motion on Route 80. Hours later, Mona pulled into the Frontier Nursing Service headquarters in Hyden, Kentucky.

4

Mary Breckinridge, founder of the Frontier Nursing Service, came out of the log cabin. "Thought you'd be here earlier."

"So did we," Mona said, climbing down from the truck. "Heavy rain followed us to Richmond, and we got bottled up around London due to heavy traffic. After Manchester, there was nothing but potholes."

Mary grinned. "You're lucky there is a road to Hyden, no matter what shape it's in."

"Yes, quite," Mona said.

"Welcome to my home, Wendover, and headquarters of the Frontier Nursing Service."

Farley shook hands with Mary. "Beautiful place you have here, Miss Mary."

"I like to call it home. Come on in. Supper

will be ready soon. We're having venison stew. Very tasty. I'm very fortunate that one of my nurses likes to hunt."

"I'll be there in a moment. I need to work the kinks out of my legs," Farley said, putting Chloe on a leash.

Several hounds of various descriptions came up sniffing at Chloe. She backed away and growled when they approached. Farley pulled on her leash, and Chloe happily followed him looking back at the other dogs occasionally. "Get along with the natives now, Chloe."

A man dressed in faded overalls emerged from a smaller log cabin and came up to Mary. He gave Mona the once over and seemed unimpressed.

"Noah, gather their bags and bring them into the big house. They'll be staying the night."

"Yes, Miss Mary."

"Noah's our handyman. I don't know what we'd do without him."

Noah grinned, showing crooked and decaying teeth.

Mona shook his hand and showed him which bags to carry. As he lugged the bags up the hill,

Mona whispered to Mary, "That man's teeth are horrible."

Mary nodded. "Dental care is the last thing these people see about concerning their health. There are hardly any dentists in the nearby towns. Travel is so difficult, and there is no money to pay for a dentist anyway. The Depression has hit these people very hard. I try to get a dentist from London here twice a year, but he hardly makes a dent there is so much need. These folks wait until they can't stand it any longer and have one of my nurses or a barber pull a rotten tooth. Mona, I'm afraid you will find the mountains very primitive."

"I'm used to primitive. I've worked in Iraq, remember?"

"Then you will understand these people are standoffish and clannish until they get to know you, but you'll discover beauty with them, too. They are fine musicians and sing ballads lost long ago in Europe. Musical scholars come by once in a while, wanting to register their songs."

"I look forward to meeting some of these minstrels."

"Let's go in. It's getting chilly. Rupert Hunt

got here last night."

"I hope he hasn't been talking your arm off. Rupert can be—exuberant."

"He's been regaling me with tales of John Swift."

"Is our cover story holding up?"

"Only Dr. Hunt knows your real identity. My staff has been told that Lord Farley is Dr. Farley, a biologist from the University of Kentucky and that you are his assistant."

"I hope no one bothers to check."

"Why would they? Academic teams come through here every year. Nothing unusual about that. Just keep your scarf on. Your platinum hair and unique eye coloring are a dead giveaway. Everyone has heard of the new heiress of Moon Manor with the white hair and yellow eyes."

"I hope we haven't put you to too much trouble."

"It's the least I can do. Your charitable contribution to the Frontier Nursing Service was very generous indeed."

"Do you believe there are lost silver mines, Mary?"

Mary looked concerned. "I don't know, Mona, but this is what I do know. People say there is more than one of these mines and come looking all the time and some are never seen again. That doesn't account for the bizarre accidents that happen. There's a lot of tragedy attached to these mines. The Indians say they are cursed."

"There are no Indians around here now."

"The descendants of the Shawnee chiefs Blue Jacket and Cornstalk come every so often looking for the lost Shawnee silver mines. What they can tell you will make your hair stand on end." Mary looked at the haze rising from the valleys and blanketing the mountains. "Enough of this nonsense. Come on. Dinner will be getting cold."

Mona followed Mary into Wendover, the headquarters for the Frontier Nursing Service with Farley and Chloe tagging behind.

A lone scream sounded from the woods.

All four people turned. Chloe's hackles rose and she emitted a low growl.

"What is that?" Mona asked.

"Sounded like a cougar," Farley said.

"That's correct, Lord Farley. It's a panther and not too far away, I reckon by the sound of her. The locals call them 'paints.' You both will find there are dangers here that you have not met elsewhere. Keep your guns close and be careful. Be very careful."

Farley and Chloe followed Mary into the building while Mona stood on the porch watching the mist roll in from the woods. She didn't like the thick woods. She didn't trust them. They were not like the wide open spaces of Iraq, where one could see for miles and miles. Yes, she was going to follow Mary's advice.

She was going to keep her guns close.

5

Mona, Farley, and Rupert Hunt sat around a large nicked harvest table as Mary dished out steaming hot venison stew thick with carrots, onions, turnips, celery, and canned tomatoes. A skillet of cornbread was passed around followed by freshly churned butter.

A lanky, black-haired man with a pencil thin mustache came from a back bedroom, followed by a woman with short, reddish hair wearing dungarees. A dog of indiscriminant sorts with brown and white fur followed and lay by the fire. He glanced at Chloe and then his eyes returned to the woman.

Rupert said, "Let me introduce Chester Combs. He's a geologist from Morehead State Teachers College and will be accompanying us."

After learning everyone's name, Chester smiled, "Hello. I actually teach music, but geology was a minor for me. I love rocks and songwriters as well. Nice to meet you." He turned to the woman standing beside him. "And this lovely lass is Althea. She will be joining us for dinner."

Althea sat down at the table. "Hello, everyone. That mutt over there is my dog, Freddy."

"I'm Mona and this is Dr. Farley."

Farley tried not to grimace and said, "Hello."

"Are you keen on our adventure, Chester?" Mona asked.

Chester unfolded his napkin. "I'm keen on collecting rock samples. I'm afraid Rupert is the only believer in John Swift here. However, if we find a silver mine, Rupert will go down in history and the rest of his group, myself included, will bask in his glory." Chester sliced a huge chunk off the butter and passed the plate to his right.

Mary said, "I'm afraid the butter tastes a little off. The cow got into some wild garlic."

Farley grabbed several slices of cornbread and passed the skillet to Rupert. "Miss Mary, I'm so hungry I could eat that cow all by myself."

Mary dished another helping of stew into a

bowl and passed it down to Farley. "Then by all means, eat up. We've got plenty."

"I'm sorry we held up your dinner," Mona said. "We thought we'd make better time. It's only 140 miles from Moon Manor but getting here was harder than I anticipated."

"No need to give it a second thought," Althea said, buttering her cornbread. She poured molasses on a plate and dipped her buttered cornbread in it. "The condition of the road after Manchester is dreadful. The county needs to fix the myriad of potholes. They are so deep, you could lose a donkey in them." She lifted a pitcher from the table. "Mona, would you like some buttermilk?"

"No thank you. I've never acquired the taste for it."

"I would like some, please," Rupert said, holding out an empty bowl.

Althea poured buttermilk into his bowl.

Farley watched with fascination as Rupert took his cornbread and crumbled it up into the bowl of buttermilk.

Rupert caught Farley staring and grinned. "You've caught me, Dr. Farley. I'm just a simple country boy. We poor folk eat cornbread and buttermilk this way to get the fat and carbohydrates we need. Simple but effective and fast."

"Sorry, I didn't mean to ogle," Farley apologized.

"When you live in the mountains, you grow your own garden and hunt or starve. We have quite the garden in the summertime," Mary said. "I know this food is not as elegant as your table, Mona, but it sticks to your ribs."

Mona laughed. "You'll hear no complaints from me, Mary. It's delicious."

"Thank you," Althea said. "I hunted the deer and cooked the stew. I can't take credit for the vegetables, though."

"Are you the cook here?" Farley asked.

Althea tensed up. "No, Dr. Farley. I'm a nurse."

Mary interjected, "Althea is one of our finest midwives. She's birthed over thirty-two babies—all perfectly healthy."

"I tip my hat to you, Miss Althea," Farley said.

"Althea wants to be a doctor. I'm sure she will make a fine one," Mary said.

"Miss Mary is ahead of herself. I have to save

the money for school first. It's hard to do so with the economy as it is," Althea said.

Mary added, "Althea will be your guide to the ridge. She'll keep you safe from the moonshiners."

"I know where every whiskey still is on this side of Pine Mountain. You'll be safe with me."

"How dangerous is it?" Rupert asked.

Althea said, "I would advise you that if you stumble upon a still—run, don't walk and stay away from any ginseng plants. People sell ginseng, and they are fiercely protective of their patches."

Mona spoke up. "Dr. Farley and I heard about Dr. Hunt's venture in the mountains, and we thought we'd tag along. An adventure of sorts."

"Uh huh," Althea said, not quite convinced.

Farley added, "I'm looking for an heirloom strain of corn native to the area. I am skeptical of Dr. Hunt's search, myself."

Rupert gave Farley a look of disdain.

Althea said, "Some adjustments will have to be made. Mona, you'll have to switch to pants because we'll be riding horses into the mountains."

"No roads?"

"Not where Dr. Hunt wants to go."

"And where is that, old man?" Farley asked, reaching for the salt.

"We will be searching for silver mines on the north side of Pine Mountain."

"Where exactly on Pine Mountain?" Farley asked, his eyes squinting.

"Sorry, I can't tell you. After all, you're looking for corn, remember?"

Farley turned to Mary. "Miss Mary, do you have a map of the area?"

"I'll be glad to loan it to you, Dr. Farley or may I call you Bob?"

Farley flinched. He hated the name "Bob."

Mona grinned and Rupert joined in, causing Farley to scowl.

Mary said, "It is very important that everyone stick to their cover story. People must not suspect that you are looking for the Swift mines."

"You said mines, Mary. I thought they were looking for one mine," Althea said.

"There may be more than one mine according to Swift's journal. Gives us a better chance of finding something," Rupert said.

"Oh," Althea said, looking unconvinced.

Rupert nodded and said, "We'll work our way across the mountain ridge until we reach Pine Mountain Settlement."

"What's that?" Mona asked.

"It's a boarding school. My friend Katherine founded it. At the end of your journey, you are to go there. Katherine will send word to me, and my nurses will have your vehicles waiting for you in London," Mary said.

Mona asked, "We're not to come back here?"

"Believe me when I say that once you reach the Pine Mountain Settlement, you'll be done with the mountains for a while. It will be best that you leave the area," Mary answered. "The more we can keep your visit quiet, the better for all concerned. Katherine will provide transportation to London."

"Is there a road between here and the Pine Mountain Settlement?" Farley asked.

Althea said, "I wouldn't call it exactly a road."

"I thought US 421 was to come through," Farley said.

"Hasn't quite made it yet," Mary said. "You're beginning to see our main problem in Eastern

Kentucky—the lack of reliable and safe transportation. There are few cars here. Most people still rely on horses to get about. The coal and logging industries have built some good roads but they are few and far between."

"Imagine," Mona said. "People still using horses for transportation in this day and age."

"I have everything mapped out," Rupert said. "We'll be following ancient warrior paths deep into the forest. The locals still use them. Current maps are not going to be of help to us."

"Charming," Farley muttered.

"I'm afraid I'm with Dr. Farley on this, Dr. Hunt. I like to know where I'm going," Mona said. "Are you strictly using John Swift's maps?"

Rupert said, "First of all, let's call everyone by their first name. I don't see the need for this formality."

"Agreed," Farley said.

"Good. Back to business. I will be referring to one of the oldest Swift maps, and I will also be using an old French trapper's map of footpaths in Eastern Kentucky."

"The terrain will have changed since the 1600s," Farley said.

"But the rock formations have remained the same. That's one of the reasons I'm coming," Chester explained. "I'm going to help Rupert decipher the maps."

Concerned, Farley would not let up. "That's the problem. A map may say 'large rock formation resembling an elephant.' That description is subjective, and there may be three rock formations in the area which resemble an elephant."

"I think I'll be able to assist with the interpretation of the maps," Althea offered. "I know all the ancient legends concerning this area."

"Do you believe in the John Swift legend, Althea?" Mona asked.

"I don't know about John Swift but I believe there may be some truth to silver mines in the area."

"What makes you think so?" Mona asked, before reaching for the cornbread.

Rupert passed Mona the cornbread skillet as she thanked him.

Farley couldn't help but notice how warmly they smiled at each other. Drats!

Althea continued. "Most people incorrectly think Kentucky's European history began with

Daniel Boone. We know Hernando de Soto explored Kentucky in 1543 looking for gold. We know Kentucky was explored by Robert de La Salle in 1669, by Thomas Batts in 1671, and Father Jacques Marquette in 1673."

"The first English explorer was Dr. Thomas Walker in 1750. That's late, but it was still seventeen years before Daniel Boone entered Kentucky," Mary added.

Rupert added, "Most people don't know this either. Natives lived in Kentucky until the mid eighteenth-century. The last town was called Eskippikithiki which they burned before moving across to Ohio."

"Why did they leave?" Chester asked.

"There are many theories. Since they burned their town to the ground, it might have been due to measles or smallpox. Coming in contact with the white man was hazardous for an Indian's health," Althea mused.

"I thought de Soto only explored western Kentucky," Farley said, grabbing an apple from a basket on the table.

"There is evidence the Spanish were through-out the Appalachian Mountains including where we're heading," Rupert said, excitedly.

Mona was interested and felt it would be a major find if they could prove the Spanish were definitely in Eastern Kentucky. She leaned forward and asked, "Based on what evidence, Rupert?"

"We know de Soto was looking for precious metals in the New World. He mined gold in Georgia. Many believe he had found mines in the mountains. Spanish doubloons have been found throughout Kentucky, Tennessee, and West Virginia."

"That's it?" Farley scoffed. "That's all you've got? Must be thousands of square miles you're talking about."

Rupert held up his hand. "Be patient, Bob. A four-ounce lump of silver was found in 1872 near a rock with the date of June 3rd, 1632 inscribed in Spanish. This was in Jackson County, Kentucky, not too far from here."

"There's a problem right there. De Soto landed in Florida in 1539, almost a hundred years earlier," Farley said.

"Yes, but the location of the mines would have been transmitted to the Spanish government by the expedition, and Spain would have sent men to work the mines or least explore for them."

Mona asked, "Do you think de Soto was looking for El Dorado?"

Chester answered, "I think that is plausible, and possibly a route to China."

Farley argued, "I'd like to know how Spain received word on these mines. De Soto died en route and over half of his seven hundred men died as well. Most of the survivors never returned to Europe."

Althea said, "We know the Spanish had contact with the indigenous people. The Cherokee say the Spanish enslaved them to work the mines which had already been worked by the Cherokee for centuries. Archeologists have discovered all sorts of grave artifacts made of precious metals such as copper axes, silver bracelets, earrings, and other ceremonial objects in native graves made long before the Spanish arrived, so we know the Woodland peoples mined and smelted ore for their own use. Even French fur trappers and explorers noted the amount of silver the Shawnee and Cherokee wore."

Rupert added, "We have a 1690 written account by James Moore, Secretary of the Virginia colony, stating that he discovered previous activity of Spanish mining and smelting near Kings Mountain, North Carolina and that the Indians claimed they had killed the Spanish miners."

"Again, what has that got to do with Kentucky?" Farley asked. "North Carolina is many miles from Kentucky."

"The Indians even used silver for making bullets," Althea said, ignoring Farley. "Jenny Wiley said she was forced to smelt silver for making bullets during her captivity."

Mona asked, "Who is Jenny Wiley?"

Mary answered, "Jenny is very famous in these parts. She was captured in 1789 by a band of braves who killed her family, including her brother and her five children. Her husband was away on business. She escaped after eleven months in captivity. She claimed the Indians, consisting of Cherokee and Shawnee men, mined ore and she helped them smelt silver into bullets. Tradition says the smelting took place under a rock shelter in Eastern Kentucky."

Rupert added. "What I'm trying to prove is that the local natives knew how to mine, smelt, and create beautiful objects long before the white man appeared. This was noted by the Spanish conquistadors who enslaved these people to either betray the location of the mines or to work them." He looked around the table. "Can we agree on this fact?"

Althea nodded.

Mary said, "I'm game."

Chester smiled and looked at Rupert, nodding.

Farley lit a cigarette, saying, "I believe the locals worked mines and made their own objects from copper, silver, and sometimes gold. I also believe de Soto enslaved them to work the mines, but on the other side of the Appalachian Mountains. Nowhere near Kentucky. De Soto didn't come this far north nor did other Spaniards years later." After receiving a fierce look from Mary, Farley took another puff and threw the cigarette into the fireplace.

"Miss Mary?" Rupert asked.

Mary laughed and shook her head. "I'm not getting into this bear fight. I have no opinion except to say it would be exciting if you could find something concrete. Personally all these dates are making my head spin. I don't know how you keep the people and the years straight."

Rupert looked around at the expectant faces sitting around the harvest table. The fire crackled in the fireplace as Mary threw another log on the fire while Althea poured everyone another cup of coffee and then cut squares in the gingerbread she had made for dessert.

"Smells lovely," Farley said after receiving a plate of gingerbread with a brown sugar and cinnamon sauce poured over it.

Mona teased, "Give *Bob* another piece. He'll agree to anything if he's fed enough."

Mary produced a jug of moonshine and poured a little bit in everyone's cup. "To keep the night chills away."

Rupert took a sip. "Lordy, this stuff will put hair on your chest. Ladies, beware." He took another sip. "Shall I go on?"

"Please do," Mary said. "I find this fascinating."

"After the Indians ran the Spaniards off, then came the French traders and later the English—that's where John Swift comes in."

"Did the French look for the mines?" Mona asked, refusing cake. She didn't care for the taste of ginger.

"Somewhat, but their main focus was establishing fur trade with the native peoples and building forts. The English came later and their main goal was to establish colonies pushing everyone out of their way, including the Indians. The Cherokee tried to assimilate but once gold was confirmed on their land, they were forced to Oklahoma via the Trail of Tears."

Chester interrupted, "I think it was Kentucky's first historian, John Filson, who initially referenced John Swift. Before Filson, the Swift mines were an oral tradition."

"That's correct, Chester," Rupert said. "In 1788, he claimed a tract of land that included a silver mine worked by a man named Swift. In fact, it was John Filson, who first told Daniel Boone of the great hunting in Kentucky. I think he also told Boone about the Swift tradition because not long after being associated with Filson, Boone was missing for two years. Supposedly he was on a 'longhunt.' However, Rebecca, his wife, thought he was dead and had a baby by another man—Boone's brother, Ned."

Mona asked, "You mean she married the brother?"

Rupert answered, "Hmm. Not exactly. Ned was married to Rebecca's sister, Martha, and both women were pregnant at the same time."

Althea pursed her lips. "Ned seemed to be quite the busy fellow. What happened when Daniel Boone returned?"

"Not much. He and Rebecca reconciled, and Boone claimed the child as his own. In fact, many said Jemima was his favorite child. Life went on, I suppose, and Daniel Boone became a legend."

"I wonder what Rebecca and Martha said to each other," Mona mused.

Mary said, "Well, it was Daniel's own fault for the confusion. Leaving his wife with no word for two years. That's horrible. I guess Ned thought he was being friendly."

Everyone laughed except Chester whose brow furrowed. "Wasn't it Boone's buddy, John Finley, from the French and Indian War, who told Boone of the Cumberland Gap?"

"No, it was Filson."

"I thought Boone and Finley went to Kentucky in 1769. Filson didn't arrive in Kentucky until 1783," Chester insisted.

Rupert insisted, "I'm sorry, it was Filson. Their names are very similar."

"What happened to Filson?" Farley asked.

"The story goes he was on a surveying expedition near the Great Miami River and was attacked by the Shawnee in 1788. However, his body was never found. I think that is a cover story. I think he was looking for the mines," Rupert said.

"In Ohio?" Farley asked.

"I don't think he was in Ohio. There have been skeletons found in clothing of that period with the initials JF found on their musket in Kentucky. I think the Ohio story is a cover."

"I don't dispute your thought process here, but 1500 Europeans were killed either by the Shawnee, Cherokee, Mingo, Creek, and other tribes. That doesn't even cover those who perished by accidents or natural causes. Muskets with the initials JF could have belonged to anyone," Mona said. "I'm not trying to be the Devil's advocate here but those are the facts."

"I am," Farley said, brusquely.

Mona continued, "I think we should use restraint. We're not sure if there is one mine or several mines we are looking for. Swift's journal has conflicting information."

"Please go on, Rupert," Althea said, giving Mona a dark look.

"The story goes that Swift, who had fought with George Washington in the French and Indian War helped a French prisoner captured by the Shawnee to escape—a man by the name of Munday. In return for Swift's help, Munday gave Swift the location of several silver mines that Munday had been forced to mine as a slave. After the war, Swift recruited several of his war buddies, and they found the mines as described, mining them from 1761 to 1769. Swift was resentful of the British, so he used the silver to counterfeit English crowns. What silver they could not carry out each year, they buried along several routes when heading back to civilization. That's what we're after—either finding any silver mine, buried silver, or evidence of Swift's existence."

"What evidence is there of John Swift's existence?" Althea asked.

"There's John Filson's mention of him in the

deed, oral tradition, and Swift left a map and a journal."

Mona said, "I understand there are thirty-six versions of this 'journal.'"

Rupert nodded. "And I've read all thirty-six. After piecing together the clues on the map along with Swift's journal, I think our best shot is the north side of the Pine Mountain Ridge."

"Are there journals or maps from the other men who worked with him?" Farley asked.

"None that I would say are reliable."

"Why not?"

"There are tales that the men began fighting one another over the silver and two even killed each other."

"Why is it only Swift who comes back looking for the silver years later?" Farley asked. "Why not the other men on his team?"

"There are various stories of what happened to Swift's partners, but the most damaging one is that he killed them with a sword while they slept in 1769 and took all the silver for himself."

"That tears it. Too grisly for me." Farley stood. "I need my beauty sleep if I'm going treasure hunting tomorrow. Good night, everyone. Chloe, come girl."

"Good night," Mona said, watching Chloe trot after Farley. "The little hussy. She's deserting me." Turning to Mary, Mona asked, "Do you have a telephone I can use." Something about tonight's conversation didn't sit right with her, and she needed to check.

"There's one in my office."

"Good, I need to make a long distance call."

"My office is always unlocked. Are you going to make a call tonight? It's late."

"I think I must, but I also need to wash this grime off. May I use your tub as well?"

"Of course, Mona. That's a good idea. The streams will be too cold to bathe in, and even a nurse's bath will be frigid."

Mona and Mary walked toward the bathroom. "We have two bathtubs. With all these females working here, we need them."

"How many nurses work here?"

"It varies, but I like to keep around twenty-five nurses at all times. Every year, I lecture at women's colleges drumming up interest. You would be surprised at the number of nursing students who are interested in helping, but the problem is that we only keep them a year or two. Life is very hard here—the isolation not to mention the hard traveling they have to do on horseback with only limited supplies to assist them. But here's something that even fancy East Coast doctors can't achieve with all their modern doodads—our baby survival rate is higher than the national average. My nurses are very proud of that fact."

"You *should* be very proud of the work you do."

"I am. I love the mountains. I'm sorry, Mona, but I'll take the mountains over the posh Bluegrass any day."

"You seem to love the people, too."

"I do. They're resourceful, independent, and intelligent. Very creative, too. They just haven't had the advantages of the rest of the country as they are so isolated. Once roads and electricity come to the mountains, things will change for the better. I'm hoping in five years my nurses won't need to see their patients on horseback. They'll be riding in cars."

Mona laughed. "Speaking of the nurses, I bet they're ready for a hot soak when they come back from their rounds."

"You bet. Mona, you won't believe this but we have two modern tubs out of five in the entire county. Come on. Let's get you soaking in some hot water and then off to bed. You'll be leaving at sunrise."

"That early?"

"You gotta make hay while the sun shines around here." Mary stopped before Mona's bedroom. "I'll see you in the morning."

"Good night, Mary," Mona said before turning the handle on the door. A good hot bath was what she needed to calm her frayed nerves. She couldn't help but find Farley's scoffing intriguing. She also harbored doubts about this expedition, but finding something of importance was Rupert's responsibility.

She was just along for the ride, but first she had to make that call.

6

There was a scratch on the door which opened slightly.

"Mona, are you awake?" Farley asked, sticking his head inside.

"What do you want?" Mona said, rising up.

Farley entered the room and crawled into bed with Mona. "I want to speak with you about this trip."

"I don't think you need to get into bed with me in order to talk things over."

Farley grinned as he scooted closer. "No, I don't. This cuddle is for me." He pressed his body against Mona's. "Ah, that feels good. I might not get another chance for a while."

"As if cuddles are your intent here. You better not grope me."

Lying on his side, Farley crooked his elbow and rested his head in his hand. "I'm rather serious, old girl. I take it that you've studied Rupert's map. What do you think?"

"It's a fake."

"Now we're getting somewhere when good sense takes over speculation. Tell me why you think so."

"The map that Rupert showed me is made of deer hide. According to legend, Swift did sell maps made of deerskin, but Rupert's skin doesn't look old enough. Also, the spelling on the map is too modern. People in the eighteenth century spelled differently."

"Why would Swift sell maps to his mines?"

"According to the story, Swift went to England to get investors for the mines so he could have a full scale operation, but this was in the midst of revolutionary fervor back in the colonies. Swift was pro-independence for the colonies and apparently could not keep his mouth shut about his opinion. That's one of the reasons he was counterfeiting British crowns. He hated Great Britain's hold over America."

"It would seem to me that he could have gone

to a rich merchant in Boston to underwrite the mining operation," Farley said.

"Too close to home. Swift couldn't risk being outmaneuvered by colonial investors who would turn on him and mount their own expedition."

"It would have been more difficult for someone living in Great Britain to double cross him."

Mona continued, "Swift was arrested for treason against the crown and imprisoned until after the Revolutionary War. However, by that time, Swift's health had declined including the loss of his sight. So he sold various maps with different landmarks in order to keep body and soul together."

Farley took a deep breath. "You smell lovely. Rose water?"

"We have to get up in a few hours. This is not the time for a little slap and tickle."

Farley put his arm around Mona. "There's always time for pillow talk."

Mona pushed Farley away as Chloe jumped into the bed and lay between them. The dog licked Farley's face.

"This animal is friendlier than you are."

"I think Chloe is telling you that it is time to

go back to your own room."

"We wouldn't have this problem if you would marry me."

"I don't want to get married. You just want to get your hands on my money," Mona teased.

"Oh, tosh. I'm in love with you, Mona, and we are wasting precious time."

Mona cupped Farley's face. "Let's talk about marriage after you've been sober for a year. I need to be sure of your sobriety. I will not marry a drunk."

Farley winched.

"Oh, Robert. I am so sorry. That was such an unkind thing to say." Mona hated herself for a moment. Why did she say that?

Farley lay on his back studying the ceiling. "I'll make it, Mona. Wait for me. Just wait for me." He climbed out of bed and quietly left the room.

Feeling awful, Mona cried softly into her pillow. She wished she didn't have to be so unkind, but it was better in the long run to state the obvious. She would not marry a man who drank. Mona had seen too many women ruin their lives after giving in to men with fatal flaws. Love was not always the best course for a woman thinking she could change the man she loved. Often enough, it *was* the man who changed the woman and not for the better.

She did love Lawrence Robert Emerton Dagobert Farley. She loved him with all her heart but love was not enough for Mona.

7

After a breakfast of buttered grits, toast, cooked apples, and thick-cut bacon, Mona followed everyone to the horses.

Althea assigned everyone a mount.

"I'm not a very good rider," Mona confessed, staring at a huge quarter horse sporting a thick winter coat. "This horse must be seventeen or eighteen hands high. He's gigantic."

"That's why you have a western saddle. It will be easier for you. If you think you're going to fall off, just hold onto the horn." When Mona didn't look convinced, Althea said, "Mona, don't worry. I'll be in the lead. Your horse will follow any-where my horse goes. Chester will bring up the rear with the pack mules. We'll travel in a straight line and take it nice and easy."

"What's his name?"

"Her name is Shaggy."

Mona looked underneath the horse. "I see what you mean."

"She's a very calm horse. A nice temperament. The two of you will get along fine." Althea paused for a moment, trying to decide how she was going to approach the next subject. "Mona, I have to talk to you about Chloe. She needs to stay here. I've already talked to Mary, and she's agreed to watch her while we're gone."

"I don't understand. She's a good dog."

"We're going to be traveling ten to fifteen miles a day over rough topography. Do you really think Chloe can keep up? She'll keep us from making good time. It's not kind to her. I mean— look at these mountains. Does she have experience climbing these hills?"

Mona looked at Freddy waiting by one of the horses. "Is your dog going?"

"Yes, he goes everywhere with me. Freddy is used to the terrain and can endure the travel and weather."

Mona thought for a moment. She needed to do what was best for Chloe though she wanted the dog with her. "You're right. I wasn't thinking. I don't want to put Chloe in danger. Everyone in the Bluegrass refers to this terrain as 'hills' but they are serious mountains."

Althea patted Mona's shoulder. "She'll be waiting for you with our people in London. It's for the best."

"I'll tie her up," Mona said, upset that she was leaving Chloe behind.

"Mary already has Chloe locked up in a bedroom until we leave. It's better this way."

Mona had not anticipated how challenging the Appalachian Mountains would be, and she didn't feel good about leaving Chloe behind, although she knew the poodle would be well taken care of. Althea was right. Leaving Chloe was for the best. Mona didn't know what was the matter with her. She had hurt Farley and made a careless judgment call concerning Chloe. Mona needed to get back on her game. She led Shaggy over to the mounting steps, but Farley, a natural horseman, helped Mona into her saddle and then quickly mounted his horse. He had barely spoken to her during breakfast, and she didn't encourage his conversation.

All the horses lined up in a single file, waiting for Althea to give the word to push forward.

Rupert looked at the guns everyone else was toting. Mona wore a pistol. Both Althea and Farley had a rifle. He was sure Chester was packing something from the bulge in his jacket. "What's with all the guns? This is not 1600 you know. No Shawnee braves are hiding behind a rock formation ready to attack."

Althea frowned. "Yeah, but there are bears and panthers."

"Bears are hibernating and panthers are not known to attack humans."

"Better safe than sorry. Get on your horse, Rupert," Althea said.

"I don't like guns. Don't see the need for them," Rupert muttered, pulling himself up on his horse.

Althea said, "No nurse has ever been accosted but mischief does happen from time to time from the two-legged varmints. That is to others—not to the FNS nurses. I mean people disappear all the time in the mountains—never to be seen again. Get my drift." She grinned impishly at Rupert.

He replied, "Yeah, I get it."

Mary stood on her porch. "Althea, did you pack the liniment for their thighs? Everyone will be awfully sore after today."

Althea waved. "I have it and beeswax salve, too. Don't worry, Mary. I'll take good care of them." She gave her horse the command to move forward, and the little caravan started on their adventure. Freddy ran ahead, barking.

"Y'all are to be at the Pine Mountain Settlement in two weeks or we'll come looking," Mary yelled.

Rupert turned in his saddle. "We'll be on time, Miss Mary. We'll notify you as soon as we get there."

They followed the paved road several miles and then crossed over a creek leading to a barely discernible footpath. Though the trees were bereft of leaves, the forest was quiet with only an occasional call of a bird or the chatter of a squirrel. Once in a while Mona caught the swift movement of a deer out of the corner of her eye, but she didn't have much time for admiring nature. The terrain was rough which made riding difficult. Mona wished she was a better equestrienne but she managed to keep her seat although she grabbed the saddle horn constantly to steady herself. Within a couple of hours, her thighs were burning and her back was aching, so when Althea stopped to give the horses a rest by a stream, Mona was beyond grateful.

Farley helped Mona off Shaggy. "Sore?"

"Quite. I've ridden donkeys and camels for long periods of time and never suffered like this. It was in the desert and the land was flat. This constant up and down these hills is wearing me out, and we've just begun."

"You'll get used to it." Farley led the horses over to the stream.

Mona followed. "Robert, about last night."

"There's nothing to discuss, Mona. You have every right to want a husband you can trust. I understand."

"I didn't mean to hurt you."

"Didn't you? I wish you would tell me if you're not interested. It's cruel to lead me on like this."

"I'm not leading you on. I just want to make sure. You say you understand and then you make useless accusations."

"You can dish it out, but you can't take it. For your information, I'm not a drunk. Yes, I do have a drinking problem. However, I've been stone cold sober for months now. I fought in a terrible war and have used alcohol and other drugs to ease my suffering when the black dog is upon me. I do not deny what I've done nor am I ashamed of it, but I have always acted with honor and am respected for both my deeds and judgment. I fulfill my duties to the utmost of my abilities. No one has ever accused me of being a cheat or unfair or imprudent. If that's not enough for you, Madeline Mona Moon, then so be it, but you are never to insult me again. I won't have it. Now, if you will excuse me, I'd like to have one of those sandwiches Althea is handing out." Farley handed Mona the horses' reins and stormed off.

Mona led the horses deeper into the stream wondering if she was one of the stupidest women on the planet. Most women would give their eye teeth even to be noticed by Robert Farley. Why was she pushing him away? Was she really that afraid of love?

Mona had never gotten over the fear that Robert Farley could break her if she let him in. Yes, she was afraid she would love Robert Farley too much and it would destroy her.

8

It was several hours until dark when Althea chose a meadow to bed down. It took an hour for Althea to care for the horses while Farley and Chester unpacked the mules.

Mona and Rupert set up camp and built a fire. Mona quickly gathered wood, started a fire, and made coffee while Rupert sliced potatoes into several skillets with country ham and poured water to make a thin gravy. It wasn't long before the other three joined them. Rupert dished out the potatoes and ham, which were gratefully accepted by all.

"Tomorrow I have to make a detour to see a patient. After that we can resume the quest," Althea said, giving Freddy some scraps.

"I thought we weren't to have contact with

the locals," Rupert said. From the pitch in his voice, he was obviously disturbed. He looked quickly at Chester, who shrugged.

"You don't have to go anywhere near the house, but I have to check on Mrs. Fugate. I promised the next time I was close I would stop in. It won't take over an hour or two. Y'all can wait down the path. Once I'm finished, we can resume. It's on our way, Rupert," Althea said, perplexed at Rupert's concern.

"It will be fine, Althea," Mona reassured. "We're being followed anyway."

"What do you mean?" Rupert said, searching the tree line.

"Don't worry," Althea said. "Someone spotted us and is curious about what we are doing. Frontier nurses usually travel alone and stay at someone's house for the night. The fact that I am traveling with others and pack mules will create some interest. Just ignore him. He'll get bored and move on. Happens all the time."

"Regardless, I think we need to take turns standing guard tonight. I would hate to have to walk out of these woods because someone stole the horses," Farley said.

"I think that is sound advice," Chester added, pulling out a harmonica from his shirt pocket.

Rupert nodded in agreement.

"Well, I'm not going to stand guard," Althea said. "If he wanted to harm us, he would have. I'm going to bed. The rest of you can stay up if you want. Whoever is following us knows me. We're safe." Althea threw her coffee out on the ground and handed the cup to Mona. "I'm turning in. Good night, everyone. Come, Freddy." She unfurled her bedroll and climbed in, turning her back on the other four.

Freddy lay beside her licking his paws.

"Good night, Althea," Rupert said, gathering dirty aluminum camp dishes. There was just enough moonlight for him to wash the dishes in the creek. Chester helped him.

Mona threw more wood on the fire. "Robert, I'll take a turn tonight guarding. I think it's a good idea."

"Did you get a good look?"

"Just glimpses. I think it's an older man. I saw a beard and gray hair."

"Could be some old codger just wanting to see what we are up to."

"We might be trespassing on his land."

"So far, Althea has kept us close to communal pathways and trails. I don't think that's it, but we are carrying two mules loaded with expensive supplies. That's awful tempting."

Mona offered, "I'll take the first watch. I'll wake you around midnight."

"I think I'll take you up on that. I'm beat." Farley climbed into his bedroll and was soon asleep.

Mona was relieved that Farley was civil to her after their argument earlier in the day. She realized she had been unfair. Maybe they could patch things up and start fresh on this trip. Mona hoped so because it unnerved her when Farley was unhappy with her. She didn't feel centered when that happened.

When Rupert and Chester came back, Mona helped them tidy up the camp. Rupert laid out what he was going to cook for breakfast and stored it in saddlebags near the fire. They chit-chatted with Mona for a while until they begged off and went to sleep.

Restless, Mona tended the fire and checked the horses and mules.

Freddy raised his head watching Mona. Sensing nothing amiss, he laid his head back down.

Petting Shaggy's neck, Mona studied the night sky and was amazed at the brilliance of the stars. "Look Shaggy. You can see the Milky Way," Mona whispered.

The lonely hoot of an owl and the distant baying of a hound sounded in the distance. Then Mona heard the unmistakable sound of dry leaves being crushed by someone walking about.

Hearing the noise also, Freddy rose and softly growled staring into the trees.

Slowly, Mona moseyed over to the fire and threw more wood on it, causing the flames to shoot upward. Making sure she was standing in front of the fire and could be seen plainly from the line of trees surrounding the camp, Mona took out a revolver and holster from her saddlebag, checked the chamber, and snapped the gun shut before buckling the holster around her waist.

"Shh," she said to Freddy. "I've got this. Go back to sleep." Grabbing the last cup of coffee, Mona sat a little outside the camp circle watching and listening.

Freddy circled three times and curled into a

tight ball on the sleeping bag next to Althea.

At midnight, she woke Farley and told him that someone had been stalking their camp. Farley grabbed his shotgun and cocked it. The unmistakable sound would alert anyone watching of Farley's deadly intent if his group was attacked. With athletic grace, he climbed a tree and surveyed the woods from his hiding place.

Mona went to sleep feeling secure that no harm would come with Farley on watch. It seemed her head had just hit her bedroll when Althea woke her. "Mona, get up. It's five o'clock. We gotta get moving."

Stiff and sore, Mona groaned and struggled to get up when Althea handed her a tin of salve. "It's still dark."

"Sun will be up in a few moments. You can see the sun's first rays peeking over the ridge. Listen—the birds are singing. That means dawn will be here soon. What do the English say— before Bob's your uncle? By the way, have you checked your thighs?"

"No."

"You better. They've likely been rubbed raw, so put lots of this salve on your skin. It may be sticky and stink, but it will save you a lot of misery."

"What's in it?"

"Beeswax, sassafras, witch hazel, goldenrod, and probably a dozen other plants. One of my patients gave it to me and it works. If you are chaffing, this will help."

"Thank you, Althea. I'll check right now." Mona drifted off into the woods to do her business. When she pulled down her pants, Mona was shocked to see that the insides of her legs were bruised and raw from riding on a horse all day. She liberally applied the salve and felt immediate relief. "I gotta get the recipe for this," she mumbled. When returning to camp, she washed her face and brushed her teeth and hair at the little water stand Althea had laid out for everyone.

Rupert was fixing eggs-in-a-basket. He flipped one of the fried pieces of bread with an egg in the middle onto a plate and handed it to Mona.

"Thank you," Mona said.

"It's a beautiful morning," Rupert said cheerfully as he dumped another egg-in-a-basket on a plate and handed it to Chester. "Enjoy the eggs this morning. Unless we buy some from the locals, this is it. The rest got cracked yesterday. I guess I didn't pack them right."

Althea said, "I'll see if Mrs. Fugate can give us some extra eggs when I visit her today."

"That would be great. Otherwise, it's canned beans and ham until we make base camp."

"Did you bring along root vegetables to make a stew?" Althea asked. "I know we've brought plenty of grits."

"Yep, but stew takes so long to cook, and we have no butter or cheese for the grits. Eggs can be cooked up in a flash while we're still on the move."

"Don't worry, Rupert. I can hunt us up a rabbit or do a little fishing. We won't starve," Althea reassured. She was beginning to think Rupert was a fussbudget and not the dashing young man she had thought he was.

Sensing Rupert was fretting over the egg situation, Mona said, "Rupert, let's go over your map again. I want to compare it to the map Mary gave Farley."

Rupert smiled. "No need. I know where we are."

"I thought you wanted my expertise. That's why I came along."

"Okay." Rupert handed his copy of John Swift's map to Mona and then dropped another piece of bread with a hole into the skillet before cracking an egg into it.

Mona studied the map memorizing the details. The features of the Swift map were so generic they could have been landmarks in Red River Gorge, Kentucky or even in Tennessee for that matter. She thought the map was useless.

She looked up when Farley joined the group. He looked fresh as a daisy even though subtle beard stubble shadowed his cheeks, making him look roguishly handsome.

"Morning," he said.

Everyone returned his greeting.

"See anything?" Mona asked.

"It was quiet," Farley asked, sipping on his coffee.

Chester asked, "What are you two discussing?"

"Someone was walking around our camp last night," Mona answered.

"I heard him, too," Althea said. "Probably the

man you saw earlier, Mona."

"You think so?"

"Yeah. Just curious, I'm sure. I've done this for two years, and I've never had any trouble."

"Well, I don't like it," Rupert complained.

"It is what it is," Althea said, handing her plate to Rupert. She moved to saddle the horses. Freddy followed briskly behind her after eating his own cooked eggs.

"What do you think, Bob?" Rupert asked.

"It is what it is," Farley repeated, rising to join Althea.

Mona smiled at Rupert. "Can you fix me another egg, please?"

"I have one egg left and your name is on it." Rupert made another eggs-in-a-basket and flipped it on Mona's plate.

"Thanks so much, Rupert." Mona took the tin plate into the woods and left it on a tree stump.

Exasperated, Rupert followed and asked, "What are you doing?"

"Making friends, Rupert. Making friends."

"We need that plate."

Mona patted his shoulder, saying, "We'll get it back. Don't worry. Come on. Althea is calling us.

The horses must be ready, and we need to put out the fire."

When Mona and Rupert came out of the woods, Farley was already pouring the coffee over the fire and kicking dirt on the dying embers. The camp kitchen had been packed up by Chester and loaded onto a mule.

Rupert and Chester climbed on their horses without comment and followed Althea on a barely discernible path in the woods. Farley helped Mona mount. She was grateful for the western saddle with its horn giving her extra leverage getting up on the large quarter horse. She put her boots in the stirrups and nodded to Farley that she was set. She patted Shaggy's neck. "I hope you got lots of rest last night, Shaggy. When we take a break, I've got a treat for you. Stole some sweet oats for you."

Farley gracefully mounted his horse which was a Morgan, whose name was Daisy which Farley thought amusing since "she" was a "he." As the others were out of sight along the path, he asked, "What were you and Rupert doing in the woods?"

"I left food for our night visitor. I learned a

long time ago that one has to treat the locals with respect or trouble will be coming our way. I'm sure our visitor was checking to make sure we are not government agents looking to destroy his still."

"Makes sense. Althea said the hills are dotted with illegal whiskey stills."

"They are making hay while the sun shines since Roosevelt has made Congress repeal Prohibition."

Farley tightened the scarf around his neck and looked at the sky. "It's getting colder. Hope it doesn't snow. If it does, I think we should call off this expedition. Snow would make the trails too slippery for the horses."

"I wouldn't think so, Robert. These midwives ride these trails in every kind of weather. Rain or snow is not going to keep this trip from going under. We'll just have to get used to the cold," Mona said.

Farley replied, "Bloody hell. I hate the cold."

"How very un-British of you since most English manors don't have central heat."

"But we do have fireplaces, Mona. It's not like we live in igloos."

Mona smiled. Farley was jousting with her again. That meant things between them had healed. Mona sighed silently and urged her horse forward with Farley bringing up the rear.

That's how Mona liked things.

Farley covering her back.

9

Althea crossed a shallow stream and stopped before a hollow that an ancient glacier had carved out between two mountains. "Let's rest the animals here and have some lunch. We're at the farm owned by the Fugates. Mona and I will go ahead and visit Mrs. Fugate. When we come back, we'll start again."

"How long will you be?" Rupert asked.

"Shouldn't be more than two hours at the most. Probably sooner."

"I'm starting a fire," Chester announced. "I'm chilly."

"I'll heat some canned soup," Rupert said.

"Sounds good. I could do with something hot inside me," Farley said. "Ladies, have a good visit. I'll take care of the animals."

"Stay, Freddy. Stay," Althea ordered her dog who whimpered.

"Bye," Mona said, glancing at Farley.

"Chin chin, everyone." Turning his back to Rupert and Chester, he mouthed, "Be careful."

Mona gave a bright smile before turning her horse to follow Althea, who was making headway up the hollow called a "holler" by the locals. She trotted to catch up with Althea. As they rode closer to the house, several scrawny-looking hounds ran to greet them, barking furiously.

Althea jumped down from her horse and held Shaggy's reins while Mona dismounted. "Don't stare, whatever you do. Mrs. Fugate is one of the 'blue Fugates.' Seeing them at first is startling."

"What do you mean?"

"This entire family is tinged blue. Now, don't act surprised."

"I promise," Mona said, excited to see her first Fugate.

"And don't talk fancy. These people speak very similar to their pioneer forebears—a sort of Elizabethan English. Try to blend in." Althea grabbed her saddlebags and handed them to Mona. "I'm putting the horses in the barn. Go to the porch. They know you're here. I'll be in as soon as I get the horses settled."

Mona slung the heavy saddlebags over her shoulders and ventured onto the porch. "Mrs. Fugate," she called. "My name is Mona. Miss Althea, from the Frontier Nursing Service, is here. May I enter?"

The front door opened and a small pregnant woman with a toddler on her hip opened the door. The skins of both mother and child were blue. "Come in. Come in. Get out of this cold," Mrs. Fugate said, cheerfully.

Mona gratefully stepped into the house, escaping the wind, and put the saddlebags on a chair.

"Please sit yourself right down in front of the far," Mrs. Fugate encouraged, pulling a rocking chair closer to the fireplace.

It took Mona a second to realize Mrs. Fugate was referring to the fire. Thinking the rocker was Mrs. Fugate's chair, Mona took a caned upright chair from a corner. "This will do fine. Thank you."

Mrs. Fugate put the child down on an oval, braided rag rug and encouraged her to play with wooden blocks with alphabet letters burned on the sides.

Having a strong appreciation for beautiful things, Mona asked, "Mrs. Fugate, did you braid this rug?"

Mrs. Fugate, sitting in her rocker, seemed pleased Mona had noticed her rug. "I did. Took me three months."

"The colors are so muted. Gives a very soft appearance to the room along with the dried flowers hanging from the rafters."

"I made it from rags I had saved over the years. I like working with my hands. You know— making something purty. I did those blocks, too. My husband made the blocks, but I carved the letters and then rubbed dead charcoals from the far into the grooves to make 'em dark."

"And that you have done." Glimpsing at Mrs. Fugate without appearing to stare, Mona noticed Mrs. Fugate had dark hair and lively eyes that spoke of a keen intelligence.

"Are you a nurse, too, Miss Mona?"

"No, I'm on an expedition from the University of Kentucky. We are collecting plant and rock specimens."

Mrs. Fugate leaned forward. "So, you're a book-red woman." She started rocking. "I always yearned for book learning. You know—so I could speak good. I can read right easy enough and do my sums, but other than that, I'm dumb."

"I beg to differ with you, Mrs. Fugate. Anyone who can make a beautiful rug like this out of rags and these children's blocks is very talented."

Before Mrs. Fugate could answer, Althea stomped into the cabin. "Hello, Rose."

Rose jumped up and offered Althea her chair, which Althea refused.

"Sit down, Rose. I'm fine. Just let me warm up a little bit."

Mrs. Fugate turned to Mona. "May I call you Mona?"

"Yes."

"My Christian name is Rosamond but folks call me Rose. My full name is Rosamond Flora Fugate."

"That's a lovely name."

Smiling, Rose offered, "I have a tea brewing. Would you like some?"

Althea said, "I would love some."

"Me, too," Mona said.

"What's it made from?" Althea asked, pulling out a pencil and paper from her bag.

"Dandelion and violet bits with some mint thrown in. It's good for what ails a body. My stomach's been tearing me up past nights."

Althea wrote down the tea ingredients. "I'm trying to notate all the local plant usage for medicine in the mountains. I think there is something to the plants they use. Much of it comes from Indian plant knowledge the pioneers gleaned and have passed down through generations. I'd like to write a book about it someday."

Rose carefully pulled out three china cups with saucers from a box and poured steaming liquid into them from a kettle in the fireplace. "These are from my great-grandmother when she first came through the Cumberland Gap. Used to have an entire set, but these here is all that's left."

Mona and Althea took the teacups and sipped quietly enjoying the fire crackling and dancing in its hearth.

Rose poured the tea into her saucer and drank it.

Mona followed suit and did likewise.

Althea asked, "How you been feeling, Rose?"

"A bit puny. I get plum worn out sometimes. Wasn't like this with the first babe. Sometimes I have spells."

Althea put her teacup and saucer on a side table before gathering her saddlebags.

"Let's see what's ailing you then. Mona will keep an eye out for your young'un."

"Of course, I will," Mona said, setting down her teacup and standing.

Althea went to the bedroom and waited for Rose to enter the room. "Be a moment, Mona."

"I'll keep watch," Mona replied.

Althea shut the bedroom door.

Mona stirred the open fire and threw on some more logs. She noticed the wood box was low, so she gathered wood stacked on the porch and filled the box. Feeling the child was too close to the fire, Mona moved her back admonishing her not to get too close to the hearth. Near the cupboard was a hand pump. Although the water was frigid, Mona washed the cups. Feeling she had done all she could, Mona sat in the rocker and perused the room.

In a corner were a loom and spinning wheel. On the far wall hung several shelves where a collection of well-thumbed books, including a Bible, and a dulcimer lay. Rose's sewing basket lay beside the rocker. She had been darning socks. Clusters of flowers and plants hung the entire breadth of the ceiling upside down, giving the room a wondrous aroma. They had wax paper or rags tied around their heads. Mona assumed this was done to catch seeds. The harvest table, side tables, and chairs, including the rocker looked handmade but were handsome, and many of the chairs had delicate carvings on the top rails. Yet, yellowing newspapers filled in the cracks between the logs, and Mona felt a draft coming from the windows.

Seeing Mona rocking, Rose's towheaded child climbed into her lap with a handmade Raggedy Ann doll and proceeded to suck her thumb while playing with Mona's hair, which was sticking out from her scarf. The warmth of the fire and the rocking caused Mona to drift off until the child pulled Mona's hair. "Ouch." Annoyed, Mona put the child down. "Play with your blocks, honey. Can you point out the letters A, B, C for me?"

Twenty minutes later, Rose and Althea departed from the bedroom with Rose buttoning up her dress.

"I almost forgot. I've got some books for you, Rose. One's a real potboiler. Got all sorts of naughty stuff in it."

Rose's eyes lit up. "Full of fast women with beautiful clothes?"

"You bet," Althea joked. "The other one's a mystery. Ever read Dorothy L. Sayers?"

Rose shook her head.

Althea put the books on the table. "I think you'll like her."

"Here are the books I borrowed before," Rose said, gathering books from the shelf. Her fingers lingered lovingly over the covers before handing them over. "The traveling library program stopped months ago. It's so good of you to bring me these here books. I'm much obliged."

"I hear rumors the government will start the program up again." Althea took them and stuffed them in a saddlebag. "Well, Rose, we've got men waiting on us, so we best be going."

Rose looked stricken. "Might could you stay? I've made dinner. It's near the noon hour. I never see anyone, let alone females. Look, I've already got the table set. Ain't no time to put on another plate. Oh, please."

"We'd be delighted to stay for lunch," Mona said, shooting Althea a pleading look.

"All right, Rose, but as soon as lunch is over, we've got to skedaddle," Althea stated.

Rose hurriedly set an extra plate at the table. She handed Mona a handwoven napkin embroidered with a red Cardinal before dishing pinto beans into bowls and pouring batter into a greased skillet. "These hoe cakes take only a minute, but you can't have beans without hoe cakes. Just not right."

Althea diced an onion and put it on the table along with salt.

Mona watched Rose expertly flip the cakes until they were a golden brown on both sides. "Rose, you need a stove. You don't even have a screen for the fireplace."

"I know but I'm careful with the far. We had a stove picked out of a Sears Roebuck catalog but the Depression hit, so it will have to wait a spell. Metal is expensive." She put the cakes into a handwoven reed basket and laid it on the table before picking up her toddler and resting the child on her knee. "I dream of electricity and indoor plumbing like folks in the flat lands. Life would be so much easier. Change will come to the hollers, though. It will come. When the government builds US 421 through here, it will be different for us in the mountains. I've just got to be patient like Job in the Bible." Rose looked at the table. "Eat up, now. Don't be shy. Sorry I ain't got no butter for these cakes."

"Explain to me what the difference is between a hoe cake and a pancake," Althea said.

"A hoe cake is made from corn meal and is cornbread. A pancake is made from flour," Rose explained, dipping a round flat cake in the pinto bean juice and feeding it to her child.

"Do you raise your own corn, Rose?" Mona asked.

"And mill it too. Everything on this table I grew. No help from the husband.

He has his own corn patch for the still. My corn is table corn. His's field corn."

"Where is the husband?" Althea asked, worried that he might have deserted Rose.

"In the hills making shine. He needs to sell it before Prohibition goes belly up locally. That's our only wages at the moment. Once likker stores opens again, won't be no need for shine." Rose turned to Mona. "I hope I don't offend you, Mona. Shine is the only way we can make money.

No one is hiring. Not even the coal mines."

"There will be jobs once more," Mona assured. "I hear Roosevelt is going to make government jobs available in Kentucky."

Rose put the child down and handed her a hoe cake. "Go play now, baby girl."

As soon as the child was absorbed with her blocks, Rose said, "Maybe fer some folks, but not us Fugates. We never leave the valley. Nothing but ridicule when we go amongst normal folks. My husband is like me—blue. I don't mind so much fer myself but I hate to see my baby abused. She has such tender feelings."

Althea explained, "She and her husband are second cousins."

"Nobody else will marry a Fugate but Fugate," Rose said.

Althea said, "We think the blue skin color may have to do with genetics, but we're not sure. Except for the blue tinge, all Fugates are born healthy. It's a mystery." She stood and looked out the window. "Rose, we've gotta go. Can we buy some eggs?"

"Get what you need from the hen house. Might look around the house as well. I let the hens out early today." Rose handed Althea some capped mason jars and a pie plate. "Take these in payment of today's visit. I'll put them in a poke fer ya."

Althea put thirty cents on the table. "Let me pay for the eggs, Rose. I know it's a sacrifice to give them up. Thanks for lunch. I'll check on you in a couple of weeks."

Mona said, "Yes, thank you, Rose."

Rose looked crestfallen though trying to put on a brave front. "Thank you most kindly for the conversation. Mona, you come again when you're in these parts, ya hear."

Mona grabbed Rose's hand and shook it warmly. "I most assuredly will. You've been most kind, Rose. A wonderful hostess." Mona turned to the little toddler. "Goodbye, little girl. I don't even know your name."

"It's Iris," Rose replied.

"Ah, a fitting name because of your love for flowers, Rose."

"She's my pride and joy."

"Let's go, Mona," Althea said, heading out the door.

Mona hastily put on her hat and coat, waved

goodbye to Rose, and followed Althea to the barn.

Rose ran after them, yelling, "Y'all be careful. Some skunk's been going up and down the mountain stealing. Taking people's chickens and hogs. Even pinching horses. Leaving folks in a terrible fright. Everyone is skittish."

"We'll keep a look out," Althea shouted back, waving.

Rose rushed inside and grabbed her dulcimer. With a light soprano voice, Rose serenaded Althea and Mona with the song *Barbara Allen* until they were out of sight.

O mother, mother make my bed!
O make it saft and narrow!
Sweet William died for love of me
And I will die of sorrow.
Father, oh father, go dig my grave
O make it saft and narrow!
Sweet William died on yesterday
And I will die the morrow.
Barbara Allen was buried in the old churchyard
Sweet William was placed beside her,
Out of sweet William's heart, there grew a rose

Out of Barbara Allen's a briar.
They grew and grew in the old churchyard
Till they could grow no higher
At the end they formed a true lover's knot
And the rose grew round the briar.

She stood on the porch with a shawl wrapped around her thin shoulders and played until her fingers ached. Rose's singing floated down the holler as Mona and Althea made their way to the stream. As the last note died away, so did Rose's happiness.

"Rose singing to us is a tribute," Althea said. "A great honor."

Mona said, "It's very haunting to hear her voice reverberate off these hills. Rose needs to move away from here. She wants more from life than making babies, growing corn, and darning socks. That woman has talent in her hands."

"That woman is in the first stage of TB."

"Oh, no!"

"How old do you think Rose is?"

Mona pondered. "Thirty, perhaps. About my age."

"She's nineteen. Life is hard up here."

Mona gasped. "Is there anything that can be done?"

"She can move to a drier climate, which would be only a temporary stopgap. The truth is Rose will be dead in five years."

"Are we in any danger of contracting it?"

"No, but once Rose starts coughing in earnest, everyone will have to take precautions."

"Does she know?"

"I haven't told her. I want to tell her when her husband is home. I need to check him, too. Sadly, arrangements will have to be made to place the child elsewhere when Rose becomes very ill."

"Will she carry her new baby to full term?"

"I don't know, Mona."

"This is awful."

"One of many horrible stories in the mountains. Besides TB, there is syphilis, alcoholism, fevers, polio, measles, parasites of all kinds— ringworms, tapeworms, pinworms. Want to help? Come back and visit Rose or write letters. Send her books. Her main enemy right now is loneliness."

Mona remained quiet as the horses plodded toward the stream where the men waited.

"What took you so long? The day's getting away," Rupert complained.

Althea twisted in her saddle and said, "Shut up, Rupert, if you know what's good for you."

Rupert's mouth dropped open. "What's gotten into her?"

Mona didn't respond, following Althea down a path which paralleled the stream.

Confused, Rupert and Chester looked at each other while Farley got on his horse.

"Come on. The day's a wasting," Farley said, kicking his horse to catch up with Mona. From Mona's expression, he knew something was wrong. Besides, didn't those dumb clucks know a man should never criticize a woman for taking too long?

Even Farley knew that.

10

They hadn't traveled very long when a gaunt man stepped out from behind a tree and blocked their path. He was wearing a patched pair of pants held up by dirty suspenders, and his frayed shirt was nothing more than the top of a pair of long johns. He had long, wispy, white hair accenting a lengthy white beard. On his head sat a battered brown hat. No jacket. No gloves.

Mona's attention, though, was focused on the man's ankle-length deerskin moccasins and the evil-looking, double barrel shotgun he held sideways pressed against his chest, not to mention the knapsack hanging on his hip. "Need help, mister?" Althea asked. "I'm a nurse from the Frontier Nursing Station."

"Watch yer dog, lady," the man said, referring

to Freddy who was baring his teeth and growling. "I hate to see such a fine animal hurt."

"Freddy, behave," Althea snapped. "What do you want?"

"You got some 'backer?'" he asked in a heavy twang.

"You asking or robbing?" Althea shot back.

The man smiled. "Asking neighborly. If I was holding you up, my baby would be pointed atcha." He patted his gun.

Farley rode up and pulled a pouch of tobacco from his saddlebag. Tossing it to the man, he asked, "How's the trail further up?"

The man took a pinch of tobacco and began chewing it while putting the pouch in his knapsack. "Get's muddier as you get to the top of the ridge. Y'all lookin' for sumthin'?"

"We're a team from the University of Kentucky searching for plant and rock specimens."

"Looking for plants in the winter? That don't seem right," the man said suspiciously, his eyes roaming the group.

"Still warm enough. Nice time to search for rocks when the leaves are off the trees," Farley answered.

"You don't say," the man said suspiciously. He pushed past Farley's and Althea's horses only to stop before Mona. He reached into his knapsack and pulled out a washed camp plate, handing it to Mona. "Much obliged for the egg, ma'am. Hadn't had one for a spell."

"You're most welcome. I didn't smell smoke from your campfire, so I knew you weren't going to have a hot breakfast. Everyone needs a hot breakfast, don't you think?"

The mountaineer nodded and stepped into the forest heading away from the group. His moccasins made no sound as he disappeared into the woods.

Rupert asked, "Althea, do you know who that man is?"

"Only by reputation. Never have met him, but by the description that man is none other than Popcorn Pearse, a notorious bootlegger. Good thing you left him food, Mona. People in these parts remember a kindness. Otherwise, we might be full of holes from that double barrel shotgun of his. We must be close to his still."

"I thought you said you knew where every still was," Rupert said, accusingly.

"Must have moved it. Let's keep on. The day is dying, and we've got a lot of ground to cover," Althea said.

Farley waited until Mona passed him. "Good instincts, my beautiful American cow."

"Oh, how you do go on," Mona said, laughing. "I do love the beautiful and American part, but can you leave out the cow? I thought we cleared that matter up."

Robert blew Mona a kiss as he pulled his horse in line after Althea.

Rupert rode after Mona, leaving Chester to bring up the rear with the mules.

Chester couldn't keep from glancing behind him. The old man spooked him, and Chester didn't think they had seen the last of him. The thick forest and the isolation of the region gave him the willies. It might be his imagination but Chester swore they were being watched. Of course, there was no evidence to support this— this supposition. Sure. That's it. It must be his imagination.

Still, Chester couldn't wait until this expedition was over, and he was home playing on his drums.

11

It was nearly dusk when Althea pointed to an abandoned farmhouse. "We'll make this our base camp. Let's hurry and unpack the animals. I don't like working in the dark."

Mona and Farley followed Althea to a dilapidated barn where they quickly unsaddled the horses while Rupert and Chester unpacked the mules. The well was dry so Mona and Farley walked to a nearby stream and carried water back to the horses while Althea set up housekeeping.

"This place is a dump," Rupert said, referring to the dirty, unkempt shack.

"It will keep us dry while we sleep. Rain clouds are heading in," Althea replied, helping Mona pour water into a washbasin. "This is an abandoned farmhouse. The owners couldn't make it here, so they went to Cincinnati to find work. They told me I could use it if needed."

"At least they left some chairs and oil lamps. I'll light them before it gets too dark," Mona offered. She placed lit lamps around the cabin out of harm's way. Mona was very afraid of fire after what happened to Moon Manor earlier in the year.

"Hey, there's even a bedroom with a bed frame and a mattress. I call dibs," Chester said.

Farley fiddled with the water pump in the kitchen. Unfortunately, the water poured out brown until after several minutes of pumping when the water cleared. "I think this water is safe to bathe in, but I wouldn't drink it unless you boil it twenty minutes or so." Farley sniffed the water. "It smells okay though."

Mona rummaged through the mules' supplies and pulled out bottles of Ale-8-One. "These are safe to drink. I brought an entire case."

"You wouldn't have brought some wine, would you?" Chester asked, his eyes hopeful.

"No, but I brought a bottle of gin and bourbon whiskey."

"You are a dear," Chester said, merrily.

Rupert suggested, "Why can't we pour gin in the water?"

"I think boiling the water is best. Alcohol doesn't help the body to hydrate. I'd like to keep the liquor as an antiseptic if needed. Many times I've used moonshine as a disinfectant. That stuff can be over a hundred proof," Althea said, picking up one of the soft drink bottles and opening it. She sniffed the contents and took a swig. "Not bad," she said.

"I think that's a waste of good liquor," Chester said, obviously put out. "Well, I'll give this stuff a try." He held up a bottle of Ale-8-One.

"I brought tea to brew," Mona said. "How about a nice cup of tea, Chester?"

Horrified, Chester asked, "Do I look like a little old lady?"

Farley snorted with laughter until Mona swirled in his direction. "What?" he asked.

"Chester, can you help me make a fire?" Rupert asked.

"Sure. I'll get some wood. It's not completely dark yet."

Althea got out the pots and skillets that they would need to make dinner while Rupert and

Chester made a nice fire.

"Mona and I have a little surprise for you," Althea said, poking through a sack Rose gave her. "Ta da!" she said, smiling and holding out a battered pie pan. "Look, Mona, I managed to keep it in one piece."

"What is it?" Rupert asked, sniffing it.

"Mrs. Fugate made us a buttermilk pie. It's my pay for coming to see her. She also gave us eggs and two jars of pickled beans. We are going to eat good tonight!"

Holding the quart jars and peering at them, Rupert asked, "Are these beans safe to eat?"

"You bet. These people know how to can vegetables. It's how they get through winter."

Farley said, "That was very nice of Mrs. Fugate. We must stop by on our way back to thank her."

"You won't be coming back this way, Bob," Althea said. "You will be going on to the Pine Mountain Settlement and back to Lexington from there."

"Stand corrected."

Althea said, "Tomorrow, I will hunt some to supply your protein needs. Mona has brought lots of canned goods, so you won't starve."

"I even brought oranges," Mona said.

"But the day after I will leave you all to continue your expedition. I will be back in nine days to lead you to the Pine Mountain Settlement."

"Why can't you stay with us?" Rupert said, flustered.

"I have patients to see. The nurse who works this area is ill, so I am finishing her rotation this month. Don't worry. I'll be back in plenty of time to get you all to the Pine Mountain Settlement."

"We have a world-renowned cartographer with us, Rupert. What was the point of having Mona along if you don't use her?" Farley said, before turning to the nurse. "Althea, we'll be fine. Just keep mum about where we are."

"No problem. Come on, Rupert. Let's get those beans heated. I'm starving and so is Freddy, aren't ya, boy?" Althea said, petting her dog."

Mona pulled fresh potatoes from a tin box. "The water's boiling. Let's throw these potatoes in and cook them. Just let me wash them first."

Chester lamented, "We don't have any butter for the potatoes."

"Don't worry," Mona said. "I've brought

steak sauce and plenty of salt. With pie for dessert, this is a veritable feast."

While the women fixed dinner, Farley kept a keen eye on Rupert. He seemed like a flibberti-gibbet—awfully fussy for a grown man. He wondered how Mona could have gotten close to such a man, although she didn't seem so enam-ored of him now. And then there was Rupert's anxiety about Althea leaving. It concerned Farley. As he understood it, Althea was a guide only. She was never supposed to participate in searching for the mines. While it was true that Farley felt a minor apprehension with Althea's departure, since she was the only trained medical person for miles, he didn't intend to get hurt, but there was always a fair chance.

Farley sat back in a chair, smoking a cigarette, and watching Mona, who seemed in high spirits. Mona and Althea gaily bantered about while fixing supper, both of them looking happy and relaxed.

Mona caught Farley gazing at her and smiled.

Chester pulled a harmonica from his shirt pocket and played Irish jigs while Rupert pulled up his pant legs and danced hitting the down-beats in Chester's tunes with his heels.

Althea cheered him on. "How do you know clogging?"

Flushed from dancing, Rupert kidded, "The dance of my people. I'm from the knobs around Berea."

Mona jumped up and tried to imitate him but failed miserably. "It's similar to tap dancing, but the beats are different." She tried in vain to follow Rupert's steps but couldn't.

"I swear, Mona. You're a klutz." Farley joined her and did some fancy dance steps he learned in the army, only to trip over his feet and fall. He sat up, grinning. "Hey, the room is spinning."

Mona helped him up. "Who's the klutz now?"

Farley grabbed Mona and spun her around, joking, "Keep up, my little primrose."

Rupert and Althea did a foxtrot when Chester switched to playing *Did You Ever See A Dream Walking?* They danced forgetting they were cold and tired, enjoying the benefits of being young and healthy.

The evening was spent cheerfully eating, storytelling, and playing music. It was a grand time for the five of them. Little did they know it would be their last happy night for evil was at the forefront of someone's mind.

12

Mona woke to the sounds of Althea slamming the front door. Startled, she raised up from her pallet near the potbelly stove.

Dressed and sipping on coffee, Farley jumped up from his chair. "What's wrong, Althea?"

"Some lowdown, thieving numbskull has stolen the mules!"

Rupert threw a cup across the room in anger. "I told you. I told you not to trust these people."

"Could it have been the Fugates?" Chester asked.

"I can't believe Rose Fugate would have any part in stealing. She's not that kind of person," Mona said, coming to Rose's defense.

"What about the horses?" Farley asked.

"They're fine," Althea spat out. "Horse thievery is considered very serious in these parts still. Out here, not having horse transportation can mean loss of life."

Chester asked, "Why just the mules and not the horses, too, Althea?"

Althea answered, "Mules are more valuable because they are steadier on their hooves than horses. Horses are considered fragile in comparison."

"Let's you and I saddle the horses and see if we can find them," Farley suggested to Althea.

"I think that's a good idea. Those mules are the property of the Frontier Nursing Service. I need to get them back," Althea answered.

Mona got up and pushed back her hair. "Give me a moment."

Farley held up his hand. "You're not going." When Mona protested, Farley said, "I'm sorry, Mona, but you not a good enough rider. Althea and I can cover more ground without you."

Realizing the truth of Farley's words, Mona said, "At least, let me fix you a hot breakfast and food to take with you while you saddle your horse."

"Sounds like a plan," Farley said. "Althea?"

"Yes, you three carry on with your exploring. Farley and I will track the mules. With luck we'll be back early."

Chester offered, "I bet it was Popcorn Pearse who took them."

"If it was, we'll hunt him down," Farley said, following Althea out the door.

Mona didn't even bother with her morning ablutions. While Rupert made breakfast, Mona filled Farley's and Althea's canteens with purified water. Then she made peanut butter and jelly sandwiches for their lunch including a bottle of Ale-8-One, two oranges, an apple, two chocolate candy bars, two boiled eggs, and a slice of the country ham. "Thank goodness we brought the supplies into the house before we went to sleep."

"This whole trip was supposed to be a secret," Rupert mumbled. "Now we've got the locals stealing from us. They know where we're camped. I think we should move our location."

"The mules could have wandered off on their own. Let's wait until this evening before we make another assessment," Mona cautioned.

"Yeah, let's wait," Chester added. "I don't want to sleep outside on the ground anymore. At least, this place has a bed and a roof."

Mona turned and rolled her eyes. If anyone had to have the bed, it should have been Althea but Chester and Rupert had confiscated the only bedroom before anyone else had a chance. She returned to the task of packing lunches for Farley and Althea and tucking them into their saddlebags. Once done, she managed a comb through her hair and washed her face from a washbasin, looking up to find Rupert staring at her.

"You really are striking to look at," he said.

"Thank you," Mona said, brusquely. Men had always commented on her looks which she found annoying and unwelcoming. She never returned the compliments but men never seemed to notice. "What's the game plan today?"

"We should start searching for certain landmarks or signage," Rupert replied.

"Like what?" Chester asked.

"Landmarks, free standing rocks, and trees with carvings of initials, names, and dates. I will give each of you a list of initials and dates to look for which we will notate in the workbook that I will give to each one of the group."

"What if we find a cave?"

Rupert answered, "Each person will receive a bag full of brightly colored ribbons to mark a pathway from the cave back to base camp. It is important that no one enter a cave alone. I think that should be a group effort with the proper equipment. I also have the newest technology—Mona bought us two metal detectors which we will use at promising sights."

"We're not working as a group?" Mona asked.

"Since Althea has to leave, that leaves one less person to explore. If she and Farley can't recover the mules, then Farley will have to continue looking for them after she leaves, which again means one less person. I think it expedient that the three of us work separately today. We can cover more ground this way. I don't intend to come back for lunch, so can you pack three more lunches, Mona?" Rupert asked.

"You two are big boys. You can pack your own lunch." Mona grabbed the canteen, saddle-bags, and her coat leaving the shack in search of Farley.

Althea and Farley rode out from the barn and came toward Mona.

"Aren't you going to eat breakfast?" Mona asked.

"Naw, if we move fast, we might find the mules," Althea said.

Mona handed them each a saddlebag and canteen. "I packed a big lunch for each of you. You won't go hungry."

"Thanks," Farley said.

"We'll be back soon," Althea said. "Come, Freddy." She nodded goodbye and rode off.

Farley lingered. "What will you do while we're gone?"

"Rupert wants to start searching as soon as breakfast is over."

"Got your compass?"

"What cartographer would be without one?"

"Don't get lost."

"I won't. You be careful, Robert."

"That goes for you, too."

Suddenly, Mona reached up and grasped Farley's hand. "I mean it, Robert. Be careful."

Farley leaned over and kissed Mona's hand. "Miss me," he said, before letting go of Mona and galloping after Althea.

Mona watched Farley until he was out of sight. Sighing, she returned to the house that was little more than a shack feeling sluggish and out of sorts. She had a heavy feeling she couldn't shake, but she was here and had better make the most of it. After all, hadn't she bragged to Dexter Deatherage how she yearned for adventure?

Mona realized that she should be careful for what she wished.

13

Armed with several sketch pads, pencils, compass, and other tools of her trade, Mona rode Shaggy east on a downward slope near a stream. Rupert rode with her a little ways, and then they separated with Rupert going west and Mona following the stream. It was her contention that early explorers would use water not only as a highway, but also as a marker if they couldn't find well traveled footpaths. Since the natives had established trading routes, Mona expected to find some trace of a forgotten path. She had read John Swift's journal where he stated that he and his men traveled such paths to Yadkin Valley, North Carolina, where several of his crew members lived. Yet she couldn't find a single trace of any human imprint from the last several years, let alone two centuries ago.

For several hours, Mona continued until the brush became too thick and she turned back, retracing her steps. Mona brought Shaggy to a stop while she made entries in her notebook, checking the time and the position of the sun. Twisting in her saddle, Mona checked her surroundings and took a drink from her canteen. She was in a small clearing. Mona looked to see if trees had been cut down or if plowing had occurred in the not-too-distant past. Finally, concluding this was a natural clearing, Mona moved Shaggy into the stream for a drink where something shiny caught her eye. As she leaned over in her saddle to get a better look, Shaggy snorted, nervously side stepping, which caused Mona to lose her balance and fall into the stream. Mona grabbed Shaggy's reins but the horse reared pulling away.

"Shaggy, stop. STOP!" Mona cried out dodging Shaggy's hooves. She let go only to have Shaggy bolt. Confused, Mona got on her knees and tried to stand up, but the weight of her now drenched clothes caused her to stumble back into the stream. That's when she saw it.

A panther! A black, sleek cat hunched down by the water's edge staring at her.

Mona gasped.

The panther snarled.

Still sitting in the stream, Mona slowly pulled her gun from its holster. "Little sister, I mean you no harm but if you make a move toward me, I'm gonna blow you to kingdom come." Shaking from the cold, Mona held the gun in front of her as she scooted on her fanny out of the stream.

The panther watched intently.

Mona's hand slipped on a rock causing her to fall backward, sending her head underwater. Mona rose from the water sputtering and flailing.

The panther, agitated by the flinging water and Mona's appearance of being helpless, let loose a scream that sounded like a woman terrified. It sprang from its position on the bank.

Mona pulled the trigger, but the gun didn't fire. She immediately reached for a knife in her boot, knowing her action would be too late. The panther would be upon her in the next second— not time enough to even raise her arm.

A white blur flew past Mona and engaged the panther into a frightful clash with much snarling, growling, and shrieking. It was a terrible struggle to behold.

The startled panther disengaged and ran into the woods.

Mona blinked. Mona blinked again, not believing what she was seeing. "Chloe? CHLOE!"

A bloody, matted poodle stood panting in the stream staring after the retreating panther.

"Chloe?"

Chloe turned and looked at Mona—her tail making a feeble attempt to wag.

Mona crawled over to Chloe. "Oh, my dear. You ran away and tracked me down. Such a brave girl."

Chloe licked Mona's face as Mona burst into tears.

Wiping tears from her cheeks, Mona struggled to stand up in the fast moving stream. "Can you walk, dearest? We've got to get to base camp. I've got to get dry, and you need medical attention. Come on, Chloe. Walk, pretty girl."

Chloe followed Mona as long as she could. When she lay down and refused to go further, Mona picked Chloe up and carried her, sometimes with the dog's back paws dragging the ground as Mona struggled to get back to the shack.

Together, they made a sad pair limping through the dense forest until Mona spied a horse coming toward her. She waved.

14

"How is she?" Mona asked, hovering over Althea, who was tending to Chloe.

"It was a good thing Bob found you when he did," Althea said. "We knew something was up when Shaggy came back."

"How's Chloe? You didn't answer my question."

"She'll recover." Althea chuckled. "I think the panther's claws got caught up in all that froufrou fur."

"You think?"

"Chloe has just a few scratches, mostly around her face, and her paws are in bad shape—almost raw. They need to heal. It looks worse that it is, though. She's mostly exhausted from tracking you down. Look, Mona, Chloe's warm and sedated. I don't want her to move about. When she wakes up, Chloe should have plenty of liquids and meat if she will take it. Give her one of these powders if she gets rambunctious. They are sleeping drafts. Just a fourth of the packet. Now, get out of those wet things before you catch pneumonia."

"Mona, listen to Althea. You're going to become ill if you don't change. I've got a nice, hot bath waiting for you," Farley said.

"A bath?"

"I found an old tub and heated plenty of water. Haven't you noticed me carrying buckets of water into the bedroom?"

"I helped, too," Chester said.

"It's waiting for you," Farley said, ignoring Chester. "It's the quickest way to get your core temperature back up." Seeing Mona was somewhat confused and still shaking from the frigid stream, Farley picked Mona up and carried her to the bedroom. "I'll help you get these damp things off."

"I'll help, too," Chester offered, grinning.

Farley shot Chester an evil look and slammed the bedroom door shut with his foot. Moments later, he threw out Chester's and Rupert's things and slammed the door again.

Chester turned to Althea and Rupert in dismay. "I guess I'll be sleeping on the floor tonight."

Althea made a disgusted cluck. She turned back to her task of skinning several rabbits she had hunted, saving the livers and the hearts for Chloe. The dog would need meat when she awoke. As she worked quietly, Althea was glad she was leaving the group. Mona and Farley were okay. She liked Mona, as she always warmed to women who had guts and determination, and even though Farley could be a bit of a prig, he was solid, but she had taken a strong dislike to Rupert and Chester. Something about them was off. Yes, Althea prayed for the sun's rays to peek over the mountain top.

Tomorrow couldn't come soon enough.

15

Farley woke to find Mona gone from the bed. Wrapping a blanket around himself, he quietly went into the main room of the house. There he found Mona spooning Chloe with her arm stretched over the dog. Both looked quite content and were snoring quietly. Farley smiled at their peaceful slumber before throwing more logs into the potbelly stove.

"What? What?" Rupert said, raising his head from his pallet.

"Just me. Go back to sleep," Farley said. "Althea and Freddy are gone. Sunrise soon."

Sleepy, Rupert hunkered back into his sleeping bag.

Chester got up and went outside to do his business off the porch. Silently creeping back inside, he saw the bed was empty and, snatching his bedroll, made for the bedroom.

Shaking his head, Farley couldn't understand Chester's obsession with that bed—nor Rupert's either. They had been positively potty about sleeping in the bedroom. Whispering between the two could be heard through the thin walls. It made Farley feel uneasy. Were those two plotting something? Putting his curiosity aside, an exhausted Farley lay beside Mona pulling his blanket over the three of them—Chloe, Mona, and himself.

It was obvious that marriage with Mona was a package deal. He wondered if he should give Chloe an engagement ring also.

16

Farley awoke to Chloe licking his face. "Here I thought it was you giving me kisses," Farley said to Mona as she bent over to give Chloe warm broth with slivered meat parts that Althea had left for the dog.

"You enthrall even the females of the animal kingdom."

"It's the females of homo sapiens in whom I am interested, especially one female homo sapien."

Mona gave Farley a quick peck on the lips.

"Ah, your breath is much better. I was going to have a word with you about oral hygiene."

"Funny," Mona replied, making a face.

Farley sat up and looked around. "Where are the lads?"

"Checking on the horses. They'll be back in a moment," Mona said, watching Chloe lap up the broth.

"How do you feel?"

"I slept like a log. The hot bath was a good idea. Thank you."

"Always worked for me when chilled, but you didn't answer my question. How do you feel?"

"To be honest, I think a cold is coming on. I'd like to stay in today and rest."

"Good idea."

"What are you going to do?"

"I'm going on a hunt for the panther."

"I wish you wouldn't. I don't think the panther is a man killer. I was flailing about and making noise. She probably thought I was prey and instinct kicked in."

"Still."

"How would you even know the panther you kill is the one who attacked me? There's got to be more than one panther in this area."

"If you rather I not."

Mona said, "Yes, don't, Robert. As a favor to me?"

"If you say so."

"I do, and now if you would attend your ablutions, you will receive everyone's thanks."

"Stink, do I?"

Mona laughed. "I'm afraid we both smell like Chloe which is an assortment of iodine, bourbon, and vinegar. Althea used most of my bourbon as an antiseptic for Chloe's wounds."

"I thought she smelled like a distillery."

Mona ran her fingers through his thick dark hair. "Got a comb on you?"

"Don't you like me looking all rough and manly? Me Tarzan. You Jane."

Mona didn't answer as Rupert and Chester tumbled into the room.

"I think it's warming up a bit," Rupert said, rubbing his hands together. "The horses are ready. After breakfast we can head out."

"I'm sorry, Rupert, but I'm staying here today and resting. I don't want to risk my health," Mona said.

Rupert's mouth dropped open. "But Mona, we're one man short. I need you. What about you, Bob?"

"Sorry. I'll be looking for the mules. Althea and I didn't have any luck yesterday. Did even see any tracks."

"You both can't do this. I need both of you or

we'll run short of our goals," Rupert protested.

"Maybe I can show you something that will ease your anxiety," Mona said. She grabbed one of her boots and reached inside, pulling out a grayish looking lump. "I found this in the stream where the panther attacked. It has markings on it."

"What kind of markings on it?" Farley asked.

"The initials JS and the date of 1663." She tossed the lump of ore to Rupert.

He turned it over in his hands, peering at it closely. "Is this what I think it is, Chester?" he said, handing the gray lump over.

Chester got out a magnifying glass, studied it, tasted it, and smelled it. "I have to do a test to confirm it, but I think this big boy is a lump of silver that's been smelted."

"Smelted when?" Rupert asked excitedly.

"I can say that this is not silver smelted with modern techniques. It is too rough looking and obviously a mold was not used. Also, there are too many impurities in it for it to be pure silver, but it is loaded with it. It's old, but how old I can't say. We could have a better idea if we could find a furnace or mine nearby."

"Let's test it now, Chester," Farley said.

"That's why you are included on this expedition."

"Very well. Let me get my kit." Chester pulled out a chemistry set from a box stored with the supplies. He scratched the lump with his pen knife after cleaning off the dirt. Carefully, he inserted an eye dropper into the bottle of nitric acid and allowed a drop to fall upon the scratch. Mona, Farley, Rupert, and Chester hovered breathlessly over the sample. This was the moment when everything was possible—John Swift was a real person who mined silver in Kentucky and all the legends were true.

The spot where the nitric acid fell turned the color of pale beige.

"It's silver! A big, gorgeous lump of silver! We're close. I knew it to be true." Rupert picked Mona up and swirled her around.

Chester slapped Farley on the back and danced a little jig.

Rupert said, "Let's weigh it."

Chester put the silver lump on industrial scales. "Just under a pound."

"Where is that stream, Mona?" Rupert asked. "We must check it out today."

"My notes are in my saddlebag. Help yourself.

It was close to where we separated."

Rupert rushed over and dumped out the saddlebag, searching for Mona's field notes. Finding them, he quickly thumbed through the pages. "This the location?" he asked.

"Yes."

"Mind if I take your notebook."

"Go right ahead. Hope you find something else."

Rupert and Chester grabbed fruit, hard boiled eggs, and the peanut butter jar.

"You coming, Bob?" Rupert asked. "Thought you wanted to look for the mules. Your horse is tied up outside."

"Coming." Farley stuffed some eggs and oranges in his pocket following Rupert and Chester. Before closing the door, he said in a very loud voice. "Mona, I cleaned your gun. It's on the table. Keep it close. Shoot three times if you need me."

Mona stood on the rickety porch watching the three men ride off—two riding east and Farley riding north. She was sure Farley was warning her about something.

But what?

17

After an hour, Farley doubled back and put his horse in the barn. Quietly entering the house he found Chloe and Mona sleeping near the potbelly stove. Mona had her gun holster near. "Mona, wake up."

Mona stirred from her pallet. "Did you find the mules?"

"I didn't even search for them. I want to check the bedroom."

"Whatever for?"

"I have a hunch."

"About what?"

"Rupert and Chester. All the furniture moving and whispering. Rupert's obsession with sleeping in the only bed while women sleep on the floor."

"It's warmer in here next to the stove. Althea

and I wouldn't have accepted it anyway."

"Come on and help me. I want to search it before those two get back.

Farley helped Mona up while trying not to disturb Chloe.

"They'll be gone for hours yet. What are we looking for?"

The two stood in the doorway surveying the room. There was a battered brass bed with a stained mattress. A Standard Oil calendar from 1931 graced the wall and an old chest with most of the drawers missing had been pushed by the bed to act as a night stand. The wooden bathtub, now empty, was turned upright in the corner of the room.

"That's what the noise was about. They moved the chest over for the lamp."

"Men don't take beds from women. It's unseemly. Rupert demanded this room. If anyone were to have this room, it should have been Althea. We are here on a lark. She saves lives, and a good night's rest is of the utmost importance."

"Neither Rupert nor Chester objected to us using the room last night."

"They didn't dare."

"I don't know why Rupert and Chester would want to even stay in here. It's cold. It would make more sense to drag that nasty mattress into the main room before the potbelly stove."

"I concur," Farley said. "So what were our fellow explorers up to?" He tore the mattress from the bed frame. Nothing.

Mona checked the one drawer in the make-shift nightstand. Nothing. She checked the back. Nothing again.

Farley checked under the calendar. The only thing the calendar hid was cobwebs.

"Maybe they hid something in the walls."

"I don't think so. The owners of this house must have been prosperous at one time. The bedroom is wallpapered and there are not breaks in the seams."

"Could be an illusion. I'm going to check their sleeping bags. Check the walls will you?"

Mona checked the wallpaper seams and knocked on the walls. Just as she thought—the walls were solid. Jumping when she saw a dark figure pass the window, Mona realized it was Farley searching outside. Resigned, Mona pulled the mattress back on the bed.

Clang! Something fell on the floor.

What in the world?

Mona picked up a coin from the floor. "Robert! Robert! Come here!" She heard the front door bang open and running footsteps.

"What is it?" Farley asked, panting.

Mona opened her hand and showed the coin.

Farley picked it up and studied it intently. "It's a Spanish doubloon."

"Look at the date."

Farley peered at the coin closely. "1672. Where did you find it?"

"It fell out of the mattress."

"Let's see if there's more. Feel for lumps."

"The mattress is nothing but lumps," Mona said, frowning.

"I've got an idea. The metal detectors that you brought, Mona."

"Rupert and Chester took them."

"Well then, feel for a slit."

"I will, but I wish I had gloves. This thing is ghastly."

"You slept on it last night."

"There was a blanket between me and it. The floor in the main room is cleaner than this thing."

"Quit your kvetching, woman. Search."

After feeling along the striped ticking of the mattress for ten minutes, Farley said, "I think I feel something." Finding a small slit in the mattress, Farley pulled out several more Spanish doubloons, four English crowns, and several balls of ore with black streaks denoting unsmelted silver.

Mona and Farley looked at the artifacts and then at each other.

"What are we going to do, Robert?"

"Are you thinking what I'm thinking then?"

Mona nodded. "Rupert and Chester are salting the finds. It was no coincidence that I found that nodule of worked silver in the water. I would have had to be blind to miss it."

"Did Rupert send you in that direction?"

"In a passive fashion. He and I parted near the stream. There was a fifty-fifty chance that I would find it yesterday."

Farley said, "That's why Rupert was so upset that Althea and I were not taking part in the search. Someone had to find that silver."

"The question is why?"

"I don't care about why. Let me saddle Shaggy, and let's get out of here."

"How are we to transport Chloe?"

"I'll carry her on my horse in a sack."

"We still can't."

"Why not?"

"Althea," Mona said.

"Althea is not even here."

"But she will be."

"We'll go after her."

"We don't even know what direction she took. What if we take off and go back to the Frontier Nursing Service?"

"I'm with you."

"And what if Rupert has a nefarious intent? He might go after Althea thinking we went to join her and finding her alone, harms her."

"He doesn't know where she is any more than we do."

"But he knows she'll be back here sooner or later. He might be waiting for her, and she will be walking into a trap."

"First of all, I don't think what is going on here has anything to do with Althea. Rupert would not harm Althea. There's no reason to. At the moment, Rupert is salting sites. While it is highly irregular and possibly criminal for an academic to act in such a way, both you and I know it is not unusual for someone to do so when making a name for himself. It's been done before. I can tick off a list of accomplished men who gave destiny a little push."

"This goes much deeper than Rupert wanting to make a name for himself."

Farley said, "Enlighten me, oh swami."

"Let's look at the facts. Rupert wanted the bedroom so he and Chester could hide their loot."

"And protect it, but I think they had nothing to do with the mules missing. It threw them for a loop, so they had to hide the money where they felt it was safe. They considered someone might be watching, so hiding the money outside was a no go."

"That's why they were upset with Althea. They thought she would be staying at the cabin while we all supposedly were searching, thus protecting their stash if someone was indeed watching."

"Are we sure Chester is mixed up in this?"

Mona said, "I doubt Rupert could have hidden the coins and silver in the mattress without Chester knowing about it. The whispering was them trying to decide a place to hide their loot. Chester is Rupert's accomplice."

"No matter what Rupert's intent is, you need to protect your name. Once we get back to civilization, cut the funding for this expedition and put the word out that you are no longer associated with it."

"I agree, but what is the expedition's real purpose?"

"Mona, this is a great intellectual exercise, but I think we should flee this fleabag joint. It will take us three to four days to return to Wendover. The horses are in good shape and shouldn't have any problem getting back. Once you're safe, I can turn around with a fresh horse and be back here in two days traveling light. That's five to seven days. Althea said she would be back in nine."

"What will you tell Rupert?"

"I'll tell him that you took a turn for the worse, and we went in search of medical assistance. If we take too long, I can leave you with Mrs. Fugate and head back."

"Okay, Robert. I think you're right. Let me

give Chloe another sleeping draft before we start. I'm going to make a sling out of a blanket for her that can be hung over the saddle horn, so you ride Shaggy. She's the strongest of the horses and can take the extra weight."

"You're going to ride an English saddle on my stallion?"

"The stallion named Daisy?"

"I'll ask you not to insult my steed."

"I'll make do riding Daisy. Let's pack enough food and water for two days. We can restock at the Fugates."

"Let's put this stuff back. I don't want Rupert knowing that we stumbled upon his stash."

Mona turned her head and cautioned Farley. "Hush. Do you hear that?"

"Bloody hell. I think they're back. There goes our plan to sneak away quietly."

Mona and Farley hurriedly straightened the bedroom and rushed into the main room.

Rupert threw the front door open. "Come quick! Chester has fallen into a ravine."

"What happened?" Mona asked.

"His horse became skittish and threw him. I think the panther was nearby."

Farley asked, "Can he climb?"

"He's hurt. If Chester could have climbed, I would have gotten him out."

Farley turned to Mona. "Stay here. I'll go."

"No. I'm coming as well." She turned to Rupert. "Fill up the water canteens and get the first aid kit out of that box there. Is Chester conscious?"

"Yes, but he thinks his arm is broken." Noticing Mona's and Farley's fallen faces, Rupert offered, "I'll make some splints."

"Help me with my horse," Mona said to Farley. "She's awfully high for me."

"Hurry," Rupert said, gathering supplies and water.

Mona and Farley made their way to the barn to saddle Shaggy.

Farley led the horse from her stall and threw a saddle blanket on her. "I don't like this."

"Neither do I. Could be a trap of some sorts. They were supposed to go where I found the silver. There is no ravine in that area."

"Make sure your gun is loaded, Mona." Farley tipped Mona's face up with his fingers. "And don't be afraid to use it."

"Let's hope it doesn't come to that."

"Are you guys ready?" Rupert asked, standing in the barn doorway.

"Just about," Farley replied, throwing the saddle over the blanket.

Mona said, "Bring Shaggy up to the house. I'll make sure we have everything. Rupert, come with me." Mona and Rupert made their way back to the house.

She asked, "Where is Chester's horse?"

"It bolted and ran off. I hope we find it. We'll need it to bring Chester back." Rupert said wistfully, "I wish Althea was here."

"If all Chester has wrong with him is a broken arm, Robert can set it. I can give him some of Chloe's sleeping drafts to provide some respite from the pain."

"Don't we have morphine?"

"I'd rather not give Chester morphine unless his injuries are critical. Morphine is addictive."

"How many vials do we have?"

"Althea left two."

Rupert looked concerned. He seemed very upset.

Mona didn't think Rupert was that good of an

actor. Maybe Chester was really injured just as Rupert said. "Let's not worry about that until we assess Chester's injuries. He could have just sprung his wrist or twisted a muscle." She put on her gun holster and checked the cylinder. All six bullets were there. She snapped the gun shut and placed the gun in her holster.

"Why are you taking a gun?"

"Didn't you say Chester's horse might have bolted because of the panther?"

"Yes. Yes. I did."

"Don't you think a gun is needed then?"

"Quite so. I'm not thinking straight. I'm so upset. I tried to get him out, but I couldn't lift him out without a longer rope."

"Where exactly is this ravine?"

"We found the spot where you found the silver. We looked around for about an hour and found nothing else, so we separated. Chester was to ride up the mountain, and I was to check down the stream. I rode in the water when I ran into thick brush. However, the stream was too cold and my horse began to suffer, so I rode to join Chester."

"So you didn't see the accident?"

Rupert shook his head. "No. Chester told me that's what happened."

"How did you find him?"

"I heard him calling for help."

"Why didn't he shoot three shots from his gun? He wears a shoulder holster."

"I don't know. All I know is I heard Chester call out for help and that's how I found him. We must hurry."

"Have we got everything we need?"

"We'll need rope."

"There is abseiling rope packed in the crate with the Mooncrest logo on it. See it. It's over by the back wall."

Farley entered the room. "Shaggy's ready."

Mona picked up the tote sack with the supplies. "Let's do this."

"Rupert, you take point," Farley said grimly, grabbing his rifle. "I'll take the back position."

"Okay. Let's hurry though," Rupert said again. "Chester is in great pain."

All three mounted and made their way toward the stream.

Mona occasionally turned and glanced at Farley. Each time she turned, Farley was further and further in the distance. She realized that she might turn again, and Farley would not be seen. He was putting space between himself and Rupert in case this was a trap. It would give Farley room to maneuver in such an event.

Mona unbuttoned her gun holster and folded back the flap as she rode behind Rupert. She wanted to be able to use the gun quickly if needed. She hoped Rupert was telling the truth. Not that she wanted Chester to be injured, but everything Rupert said was suspect.

She prayed she and Robert weren't about to fall victim to Rupert's subterfuge.

18

Rupert turned in his saddle. "Where's Bob?" he asked, alarmed.

"Don't worry," Mona assured. "He'll catch up."

"I'll need him to help with Chester."

Losing patience, Mona barked, "Move along, Rupert. We're almost at the spot where I found the silver." She reached down for her gun, but Rupert didn't seem to notice.

Agitated, Rupert moved his horse into the rushing water. "This is where we parted. Chester went up the mountain and I headed downstream. We were supposed to meet back up here in an hour. When I came back to this spot, Chester never showed up, so I went looking for him. That's how I heard him call out."

Mona quickly moved Shaggy across the stream onto the other side. "Rupert, get your horse out of the water. It's too cold for him."

"Yes. Yes, you're right," Rupert muttered, moving his horse past Mona. "This way. Stay close."

Mona and Rupert started climbing up the face of a ridge until Shaggy began breathing heavily.

"How much further?" Mona asked.

"Not too far. We should be close. I marked a tree."

"This is too rough on the horses. If Chester wandered up this way, no wonder his horse threw him."

"Chester said it was the panther, which caused the horse to bolt."

"Yeah, right.

"What did you say, Mona?"

"I'm going to walk my horse," Mona replied, hopping off Shaggy and leading her.

Rupert stayed on his horse and rode a little further up the mountainside leaving Mona behind.

She moved cautiously upward, looking carefully for any sign of an ambush. "Robert, I hope you're behind me somewhere," she mumbled, following what only could be described as a deer trail.

"Mona! MONA!"

Mona dropped Shaggy's reins and ran up the pathway.

Rupert was standing on the ground with his back to her looking down at something. His horse was grazing nearby.

"Rupert, move."

Rupert stepped aside and, in doing so, exposed a crumbled body lying across the deer path.

Mona rushed to the body and felt for a pulse.

"Is Chester okay? He must have climbed out on his own."

"No, he's not. Chester is dead. A nice bullet hole in the back of the head." Mona pulled out her gun and turned to Rupert. "Get on your knees with your hands behind you."

"What?"

"Do it."

"I don't understand. What's gotten into you?"

"DO IT!" Mona screamed.

Rupert gingerly got on his knees and folded

his hands at the back of his head.

Holding her gun on Rupert, Mona searched Chester's pockets, finding English crowns. She held them up to Rupert.

"What are those?"

"Quit acting dumb. You know what they are," Mona said, reaching inside Chester's jacket and discovering his empty shoulder holster. "You have his gun, Rupert?"

Rupert's eyes widened as he shook his head. "It wasn't me. I swear it. It was just as I said. I found him in a ravine. Check his arm, Mona. Chester said he broke it. He must have climbed out on his own. He must have!"

Mona inspected Chester's arms. "His left arm might be broken. Even if it's sprung it would have hurt—I'll give you that. I'm asking you again. Do you have Chester's gun?"

"No. No. I swear it. If his left arm is broken, then he couldn't have reached for his gun. Chester was left-handed."

"Like I believe that. Stand up."

Rupert stood, trembling like a leaf in the wind. "Don't you see that his holster is on his right side?"

"Pull out your pockets."

Rupert complied. "Mona. Mona. Listen to me."

"Take off your jacket and boots."

"It's cold."

"Do it, Rupert. I'm not kidding. I'll shoot where you stand."

Rupert took off his jacket.

"Throw it over to me on the ground," Mona demanded.

Rupert threw it.

Keeping her gun trained on Rupert, Mona stooped down and picked the jacket up. "Now your boots."

"It's freezing," Rupert complained.

Mona waved her gun at him.

Rupert sat on the ground and pulled off his boots.

"Throw them toward me."

Rupert complied.

"Now, take down your pants and lift your shirt."

"I will not. You must be mad. The wind is cutting through me now."

"As soon as I see you are not carrying a gun,

the sooner you can get your jacket and boots back."

"Very well, but this is straight out of a Tom Mix movie." Rupert unbuttoned his pants and lowered them while turning around and lifting his flannel shirt.

Satisfied, Mona motioned for Rupert to pull his clothes together while she checked his jacket and boots. Nothing. Finding his wallet, Mona threw his jacket back, but kept the boots. She checked the wallet's contents. No ID and just a few dollars. She threw the wallet back to Rupert.

"Glad to see that you are coming to your senses finally."

"Sit over by that tree and don't move."

After Rupert sat near a massive elm tree, Mona put her gun away and went over to Shaggy, who was now grazing near Rupert's horse. Gently, she gathered the reins of both horses and tied them to a low branch of a nearby sapling. Keeping an eye on Rupert, she searched Rupert's saddlebags. Nothing there but food, writing pads, maps, compass, and binoculars. No gun. Nothing that even looked like a weapon. Mona turned to Rupert. "Why did you kill Chester?"

"I didn't, you daft woman. How many times do I have to tell you? Someone else killed him. Listen to me—did you find his wallet?"

"No."

"And it wasn't on me and not in my saddlebags. Someone came along, helped Chester up the ravine, and then stole his gun and wallet before killing him. Listen to reason, woman."

"Where's Chester's horse? If his horse bolted then it should have returned to base camp, but it never came back because someone stole it."

"You helped Chester up, took his gun, shot him, stole his wallet, threw it and the gun away."

"What would have been my motivation?"

"Rupert, the game is up. I've been on to you for the longest time. You made too many errors in your little history lesson at Wendover. I know academics. Been around them most of my life. I am one myself, and one thing I know is that our kind is very particular about dates and names. You made stupid errors. You're no history professor. You're not even Rupert Hunt, I bet."

"I am Rupert Hunt."

"That night at Wendover, I made a call to my lawyer, Dexter Deatherage and told him of your blunders, and that I was suspicious. He was to call the president of the University of Kentucky that very night. If he found that my reservations were true, he was to mount a search group and follow me into the mountains. I expect that he talked to the real Dr. Hunt in Lexington and discovered that you were not he."

Rupert's eyes narrowed and his face took on a defeated look. "What gave me away?"

"You said the last Shawnee town in Kentucky was Eskippakaithiki burned in 1754. It wasn't. It was Lower Shawnee Town abandoned in 1758 near the Ohio River."

"So what. A minor trifle."

"Then you said it was John Filson, who introduced Daniel Boone to Kentucky. He didn't come to Kentucky until 1782. Although it may have been Boone's buddy, John Finley, who regaled Boone with stories of Kentucky since he had been there trading with the Indians, Boone first went to Kentucky with his brother, Squire, in 1767. It was not Filson or Finley. You got both the people and the dates wrong."

Rupert shrugged. "So I'm a terrible historian."

"I've been wondering this entire trip why all

the subterfuge. What could you possibly hope to gain with this fake expedition? Then it came to me. Everything about this trip is a red herring. John Swift, the mines, the attempts to salt findings. I have only myself to blame. I've been hoisted upon my own petard."

"Let me go, Mona, and I'll tell you everything you want to know."

"That sentence doesn't even make sense. If I let you go, Rupert, how will you be able to explain? You won't be here. Silly thing to say. No, you will tell me now."

"What if I don't," Rupert said, defiantly.

"Then I shall take your horse, your compass, maps, and your boots. You can walk out of these mountains in your socks. However, without a compass, you'll be lost since I doubt you know how to navigate your location by the sun or the stars. You'll wander aimlessly until you die from a slow, lingering death due to starvation. Perhaps someone will find your bones a few years from now. Of course, the panther can always find you, and you'll be her supper."

"If you were suspicious, why did you follow me into the mountains?"

"Deatherage never returned my call. Either he couldn't verify the identity of Rupert Hunt before we left or the telephone lines went down between here and Lexington. Remember, there was a horrible rainstorm that day. I didn't get to Wendover until late. So, I was left to ferret out the truth myself."

"If you're so smart, what do you think is going on?"

"It's a scam of some sort. Were you salting the finds so I would invest more to underwrite this scheme?"

Rupert snorted in derision. "You really are a dumb blonde."

"Okay, I'm a dumb blonde. Enlighten me."

"I will since we're alone. It will be your word against mine. That's the funny thing about this—I didn't kill Chester. I don't know who killed him, but I have my suspicions."

"Hmm. Not that I believe you."

"Chester had a gun. I never have had one on this trip. Never even owned one in my life, so if Chester felt threatened why didn't he use it on me, Mona?"

"You overpowered him and threw it away."

"Chester was a much bigger man than me. I would have had to get the gun from the holster inside his buttoned up coat. Even with a broken wing, Chester could have easily thrown me to the ground. Let's say I did overpower him and got the gun. He would have been facing me. You said he was shot from behind. So according to you, I grabbed the gun while facing him and then ran behind to shoot him. Doesn't make sense."

Mona hesitated. She couldn't deny Rupert's assessment of the murder.

"I didn't hurt Chester. It was as I said it was. I found him. He was in the ravine. I didn't have a long enough rope, and he said he couldn't climb out. He said he felt dizzy. I came back to base camp for help. Someone came along, got Chester out, and then shot him when Chester wasn't looking and robbed him."

"For what purpose, Rupert?"

"The same reason the mules were stolen."

"Why didn't they take the horses, then?"

"Maybe they couldn't. Maybe they didn't want to leave us stranded yet, but look around. Chester had a ten-dollar and five-dollar bill in his wallet. In these desperate times, that is a motive for murder. I bet Popcorn Pearse did it."

"If this was a robbery, why didn't they take the English crowns? They're silver."

"Where are you going to spend them? The crowns are a direct link to the murder, but not the paper money."

"Silver can always be melted."

"Questions would have been asked about where the silver came from."

Mona thought for a moment. "What was the purpose of the salting?"

Rupert hung his head and sighed. "I guess it doesn't matter anymore."

"Why was Chester helping you?"

"I paid him to help me. I told him it was to string you along so you would underwrite future expeditions. Chester needed funding for several of his pet academic projects, so he consented."

"You conned Chester into conning me."

"That sizes it up just about. I was plucking two pigeons."

"For what purpose?"

Rupert nervously paused, straining to hear a horse approach. Just a sharp breeze and the occasional chattering of a squirrel could be heard.

Satisfied that they were alone, he said, "It was to keep you actively engaged and interested. To keep you at least two weeks in the mountains without any communication with the outside world."

Mona stared keenly at Rupert. "In essence, you kidnapped me without my knowing it."

Rupert nodded.

"How clever of you."

Rupert smiled. "It was an ingenious plan, wasn't it? It still is a great plan! The victim is whisked away on a false vacation of sorts, only to return home discovering that a ransom had been issued for her 'safe return.' No anxiety for the vic. No emotional damage done."

"I suppose a ransom has been asked for me."

"My partner should have already received it in exchange for *your* safe return." Rupert sneered a greasy little grin.

"You'll go to jail."

"No, I won't, Mona. How can I be charged with kidnapping when you were never kept against your will? I won't admit to anything, and you can't prove I was part of the scam. The most the police will be able to prove is that someone took advantage of your absence."

"The salting."

Rupert shrugged. "A practical joke."

"Then fraud."

Rupert shook his head. "The worst you can get me on is impersonating another person, but you won't squeal to the cops. It would get into the newspapers and make you look like a fool, plus it would be bad publicity for your friend, Mary Breckinridge. People like you and she don't favor publicity. Yeah. You'll keep this quiet. I'm counting on it." Rupert took out a cigarette from his pocket and lit it. He took a puff. "I'll get away with this and the money, too."

"Not on your life."

"What are you going to do about it?"

"You're going to go down for murder! You're forgetting Chester."

Rupert jumped up with the cigarette dangling from his mouth. "I tell ya I didn't have anything to do with Chester's murder."

"This is going to get in the papers, whether you or I like it or not. You will be exposed for what you are. As soon as Robert catches up, we are going to load Chester's body on your horse and head down the mountain. Everything will come out."

"There will be a scandal."

"Yes, there will be."

"It will be my word against yours."

"Nobody is going to believe a grifter like you."

"We have to get down the mountain first. I've been telling you that someone has been following us. Chester confided in me that he felt uneasy. He kept seeing flashes of color in the woods. We are in danger. Listen, Mona, I'm not your enemy. I don't like violence. It's not my style. I'm in for the long con. I like fooling people. I don't like hurting them."

A rifle shot sounded in the distance.

"What was that?" Rupert said, excitedly.

"Shut up," Mona demanded. She waited for two other shots, which signaled an SOS.

Another shot sounded.

Rupert shot Mona a glance. "That's from a different gun."

"That's Robert's pistol firing back. Someone is shooting at him."

Another rifle shot sounded in the distance.

Mona shoved her gun into its holster and ran to Shaggy. She had difficulty mounting the big horse, but finally managed to right herself in the western saddle before spitting out these words, "If Robert's hurt because of you, you had better run, Rupert because I'll find you and kill you myself." She kicked Shaggy, and they started toward the sound of the shots down the mountain.

Rupert hurriedly put on his boots where Mona had dropped them. "Slow down. Don't rush. It may be a waylay!" he cried out, but Mona was already gone.

Mona heard Rupert but paid no mind. All she could think of was that her man was in danger. *If we get out of this, I'll marry you, Robert. I swear I will,* she thought, pushing tree branches from her face while galloping toward the sound of the shots.

After several fraught moments, Mona slowed down, making her way deep into the woods toward where she thought the shots had occurred. Finding a trail of horse prints in the soft forest loam, Mona followed them until she came to rock outcrop where a man stood over a prone body.

It was Farley lying on the ground not moving. He was hurt—or worse!

Mona pulled her gun out.

Hearing Shaggy whinny, a man swirled around with his double barrel shotgun pointed at Mona.

It was Popcorn Pearse!

19

"Put your shotgun down, Pearse."

"Who has more fire power here, little missy? If'n I shoot, I'll plumb git you and your horse to boots. If'n you shoot, you have only a wee chance of hittin' me with that little revolver of yur'un."

"I'm not backing down. Put down your shotgun."

"I'm trackin' the polecat who stole my likker and busted up my still." Pearse spit tobacco juice upon the ground.

"Says you."

"Reckon we got ourselves a Mexican standoff then."

Farley groaned and shifted slightly.

"What did you do to him?" Mona asked. She

desperately wanted to get to Robert.

"Hurd the shots and came to see. Found him this-a-way. This yor'n man?"

"Yes." Mona waved her gun. "Stand away from him."

"I'll not fight a woman who wants to help her man. You did a kindness for me. I haven't forgotten but beware, little missy. There are other varmints in the woods. I've been followin' 'em." Pearse raised his shotgun, turned, and swiftly disappeared into the woods.

Mona jumped off Shaggy and ran over to Farley. "Dearest, what happened?" She raised a water canteen to his lips from which Farley gratefully sipped.

Sitting up with Mona's help, Farley said, "Caught the trail of someone riding one of our mules. Was following him following you. Thought I would sneak up on him and then, whammy, a shot rang out. I thought I saw him through the trees. Took my best shot but he bested me. I guess I wasn't as quiet as I thought."

Mona ripped off part of her undershirt and wrapped it around Robert's head.

"Ah, Mona, you're literally giving me the shirt

off your back."

"You must be all right if you're teasing. It's just a flesh wound. Looks worse than it is."

"Will you kiss my boo boo and make it go away?"

Mona grabbed Farley and hugged him tightly. "My darling. When I saw it was you lying there, my heart practically leapt out of my chest."

"My word! Darling and dearest—two endearments in the space of a minute. I must injure myself more often. You haven't been this sweet to me in months. Did I hear you say that I was your man or was that a dream?"

Mona pushed Farley away. "You were conscious the entire time."

"I was—how do you Americans say—playing possum."

"Ugh, you disgust me sometimes. Were you going to let that man shoot me?"

"Popcorn had no intention of shooting you. He is obliged to you for your small kindness. Besides, it wasn't Popcorn who shot me. It was someone with a rifle."

"That's what it sounded like to me."

"Popcorn carries a shotgun."

"A big one."

"Two distinctly different guns. I believe Popcorn when he said he was chasing someone who stole his moonshine."

"Let's look at this logically. Althea has a rifle. You have a rifle and a pistol. I have a revolver. Chester had a revolver but it is missing from his shoulder holster."

"Besides Rose Fugate and Popcorn Pearse we have had no contact with anyone on Pine Mountain. And there is Althea leaving the group on a supposed-errand-of-mercy."

Mona scoffed. "Surely, you don't think Althea has anything to do with this."

"She's a masterful shot and a natural horse-woman who knows every cow and deer path in these woods."

"Sorry, she doesn't add up. What would be her motive?"

Farley shrugged. "Couldn't guess. If not Althea, then Rupert."

"I don't think so, either. I'll tell you about him later. It's a real humdinger of a tale."

"It's Althea, then."

"It's not. Got to be an unknown person involved. I won't believe it of her."

"Just like you didn't believe betrayal from Jetta."

Mona frowned. "That's a low blow, Robert."

"Let's not quarrel, Snookums. Help me up."

Mona helped Farley stand. "How do you feel?"

"A bit shaky. I could do with an aspirin or two. I'll manage, though." He cuffed Mona's chin. "Don't look so serious. I'm fine."

"We need to get off this mountain."

"I quite agree."

"We need to start now and travel all night if possible."

Farley peered at the sky. "Day's mostly over. We'll start at daybreak."

"No, Robert. We need to move now. Chester is dead. He's been murdered."

"What?"

"He was shot in the back of the head."

"We would have heard the shot. Sound travels long distances in these hills."

"I think it was at close range. It looked like an execution."

"Was he in the ravine as Rupert said?"

"No, we found him sprawled across the path. There were signs of a scuffle and Chester had been robbed. His horse is missing."

"Maybe the two lads had a parting of the ways. Sounds awfully like how James Harrod was murdered. Wouldn't it be something if they discovered John Swift's mine, and Rupert killed Chester over the secret." Farley looked about. "By the way, where is Rupert?"

"Long gone by now. As soon as I heard the shots I left him. Look, there's lots to tell you, but we need to get moving."

"We don't know where our shooter is, luv. Perhaps we should move north across the mountain to the Pine Mountain Settlement."

"I'm not going to leave Chloe. We must head back to base camp."

"If this fellow has been stalking us, he'll know about your attachment to the dog."

"I'm not going to abandon her." Mona strode over to Shaggy. "I'll find your horse. Don't move."

"Where am I going to go?" Robert watched Mona ride off. *I'm going to marry that wildcat if it's the last thing I do. Lord help me when I finally catch her,* he thought.

20

Mona and Farley hurried to the shack they called base camp. They waited in the tree line observing the house before they decided it was safe to proceed.

Farley pulled his pistol out and cocked back the hammer.

Mona did the same with her gun.

Cautiously, they approached the house.

Taking hold of Daisy's mane, Farley leaned over and pointed at the dirt pathway leading to the house. "Look, Mona. Tracks."

Mona followed Farley's gaze. "And wagon wheels, too. It looks like Chester was right. Someone was following us." She jumped off Shaggy and ran into the house.

Farley followed. "Mona, stop. Be careful."

Mona threw the door open. "Chloe. Chloe!" The poodle was nowhere to be seen. "Robert, they took my dog!"

"Mona, calm down. What would anybody want with an injured dog? Maybe Chloe ran out when our vultures entered." Farley looked about the room. "Mona, we have a greater problem than finding your dog."

Tearful, Mona said, "WHAT?"

"Someone has taken all our provisions. Look about. They have taken every scrap of food we had."

Flummoxed, Mona replied, "Our tools. Our clean water. Our medical kit. They even ripped out the potbelly stove and the hand pump."

"It has to be more than one person. No one man could do this by himself in this short amount of time. It took the five of us over an hour to unload."

"The thieves must be close by. A wagon can't move in this terrain fast."

Farley added, "One thing is certain. They are determined not to leave any witnesses."

Mona swirled around. "What was that? I heard something."

Farley put his finger to his lips and then pointed at the closed bedroom door. He gingerly stepped over to the door, pointed his gun, and threw the door open.

To both Mona and Farley's surprise, there stood Chloe on the filthy cotton pinstriped mattress wagging her tail.

Mona rushed over and hugged Chloe. "Oh, thank goodness, you are safe."

Farley refrained from making a face. He was glad Mona had a tender heart, but at the moment, he was more worried about their safety rather than the dog's.

A shot sounded in the distance.

"That sounded close."

"Robert, perhaps we should make a stand here."

"I've got twenty bullets for my pistol not counting my rifle. How many do you have?"

"Just about the same."

"We don't know how much ammunition our thieves have or how many there are. There could be five of them for all we know. We can't fight those odds. What if they try to starve us out? We have no water and no food. How will we protect our horses? If I were them, I would take the horses and leave one man to guard the house to mow us down when we try to escape."

Another shot echoed off the hills.

"Getting closer."

"Too close. Whoever killed Chester is still out there."

"I bet they are shooting at Rupert. It's gotta be him. I don't hear any returning fire. I never thought I'd root for him, but I am."

"At least, he's distracting them for now. We need to leave fast. I'm going to the barn to see if they left the horses' feed. Be ready to go in a few minutes. See if you can find anything."

Farley ran to the barn while Mona searched the house. Everything had been stripped. There was nothing of value to take.

Mona coaxed Chloe out from the house and waited with her on the front porch.

Farley hurried back, looking disgusted. "They even took the grain and oats for the horses. These thieves never intended us to leave this mountain—alive."

Another shot sounded.

"They are backtracking and getting closer.

Let's go," Farley said.

"Can Chloe walk?"

"Not for long. She's still pretty weak."

"Then it makes sense for you to take Shaggy and hold Chloe. You weigh much less than I."

"How am I to hold her?"

"Do you have a tote sack in your saddlebag?"

"Why didn't I think of that?" Mona rummaged through her saddlebag and found the sack.

Farley helped Mona mount and then slipping Chloe in the sack with her head exposed, lifted her to Mona. The dog whimpered and snapped at Mona.

"I know it's uncomfortable, Chloe, but we've got to go." Mona pulled the sack over Chloe's eyes. "I wish I had her sleeping powder, at least," Mona said to Farley.

"We're doing the best we can, Mona. Come on, old girl, chin up and all that."

"You're right. Let's hurry."

Farley mounted Daisy, and reaching for Mona's hand, pressed it for a moment. His unshaven handsome face was ravaged from dirt, blood, and worry. "Whatever happens, you keep on going. Understand?"

Mona nodded.

Farley took one of Shaggy's reins while Mona tied the loose one around her saddle horn, so she could hold on to Chloe. Gently, Farley led the way down the path, hoping whoever was stalking them would stop for the night while they made their escape.

But it was not to be.

21

After three hours, Mona pulled on the rein. "Robert, please stop. My arms are numb. Chloe won't stop squirming."

Farley jumped off his horse and relieved Mona of Chloe, gently laying the dog on the ground. Chloe shook off the sack and urinated on the spot.

"A potty break is a good idea," Farley said, chuckling. "Excuse me, ladies." He handed the reins to Mona and hustled behind a tree. When he returned, Mona was sitting beside Chloe, stroking the dog's back. "How are you doing?"

"I'm worn out. I don't think I can carry Chloe much longer. I need some sort of a sling for her."

Farley looked at the poodle lying beside Mona and panting heavily. He looked at the sky. "We'll rest here about an hour before we proceed. The horses need a break. By that time, the moon should arise. Help us to see."

"How long before you think we should get to the Fugates?"

"Maybe before dusk tomorrow if we travel straight through."

"I'm thinking the day after tomorrow. If we push the horses too hard, they won't last."

"I know, Mona, but this is a race. We might have to ride the horses until they collapse. Let's hope Rupert leads our thieves on a merry chase away from us."

Mona knew not to argue with Farley over such matters. He was a practical realist. Sometimes hard decisions had to be made in order to survive, and she would make them when the time came. Right now, she needed to take a break.

The rest would come later.

22

"Mona, wake up. It's time to go."

Mona fluttered open her eyes. "I must have drifted off. What time is it?"

"About nine. The moon has risen."

Mona pulled her coat tighter about her. "It's so cold."

"You'll warm up after we start riding again."

She turned to Chloe who was asleep beside her. "How's she doing?"

"She's sleeping. I'll take her next. Give you a respite."

"Chloe needs water."

"I found a small spring. I filled the canteens from it." Farley held out a canteen. "You want to try it?"

Mona shook her head. "I'll hold out as long as

I can. We can get sick due to the water. I saw English soldiers die of cholera in Iraq from drinking bad water. They called it the Blue Death."

"It should be all right coming from a spring. Besides, there hasn't been a cholera outbreak in the United States in over twenty years. Mona, you're being overly concerned. We need water."

"Dysentery then."

"And you travel overseas with these concerns? How did you ever manage?"

Mona pouted. "Make fun of me if you will, but I'm always careful of food and water. Much of the water in the mountains is contaminated due to the coal mining. I won't drink it unless I have to."

"I haven't seen any evidence of coal mining around here. We may have to take our chances. Let's see if Chloe will take some water. Regardless, she needs to stay hydrated." Farley cupped water in his hand and nudged Chloe. She opened her eyes, smelled his hand, and licked up the water. "That's a good sign. Well, I'm thirsty. Here goes nothing." Farley took a big swig of water from the canteen.

"I'll drink when I get to the Fugates." Mona struggled to get up. "Help me. I'm so stiff."

Farley pulled Mona to her feet.

Mona bent over in pain. "The inside of my legs are rubbed raw. I wish I had Althea's salve."

"Can you get on Shaggy?"

"I'll try." Mona smiled encouragingly at Farley. "Chin up and all that?"

"Good lass. I'll take Chloe."

"Are you sure?"

"Yep."

Mona held Chloe as Farley mounted and then lifted Chloe to him. He opened his coat and pressed the dog against his chest.

"Will you be warm enough?" Mona asked.

"We'll be toasty."

Mona tried to mount Shaggy but cried out.

"What is it?" Farley asked, alarmed.

"I feel like my skin is ripping. I think I'm bleeding where it's so tender."

"You've got to tough it out." Farley held Shaggy's bridle. "Come on. We've got to get off this mountain."

With tears streaming down her face, Mona gave one last groan and mounted Shaggy. She patted the horse's neck, trying to reassure the animal who was sensing Mona's anxiety. "Not your fault, baby. Not your fault."

Farley took one of Mona's reins as before to lead Shaggy in the dark. With only the moonlight to guide Farley, they made slow progress.

The deliberate, steady plodding of the horses and the cold lulled Mona to drift off. Twice she caught herself almost falling out of the saddle. She wondered how Farley managed to keep going.

Finally, Farley stopped. "Take Chloe, Mona. I'm done."

Mona rode her horse parallel to Farley as he handed the dog over to her.

He dismounted and then retook the animal. "Next time, get a smaller pet. Chloe weighs a ton."

"Is Chloe dead?" Mona asked, fearfully. "She isn't moving."

"Naw, my queen, she's asleep." He put his ear to her snout. "Listen, you can hear her breathe. Must be a deep slumber."

Mona sighed with relief. "That's good, isn't it?"

"I would think so. If she could get a couple of days of rest and food, she'd be right as rain."

"Where are we? Why are we stopping?"

"I've got to get some shut eye, and the horses need to rest. It's a couple of hours until daybreak. As soon as the birds start to sing, we'll move on." Farley moved behind some boulders. "This is a good place to rest. No one will be able to spot us here."

He lay down on the hard ground. "Come on, lass. We've got to keep each other warm. It's colder than a witch's teat."

Mona lay beside Farley as he placed Chloe between them. She was so tired she didn't think of her bleeding thighs, or that she was thirsty, or becoming dizzy from not eating, or that she was nearly done in from exhaustion. All she could think about was that she would be at the Fugates' house tomorrow where she would be warm and her belly full. And most of all, she and Farley would be safe and this nightmare would be over.

Perhaps, Dexter Deatherage had sent a rescue operation on ahead, and they would intercept Farley and her early in the day.

She hoped so. She fervently hoped so.

23

Mona jerked awake. Something was wrong. The sun was too bright in her eyes. "Oh, my God! Wake up, Robert. We overslept. The sun's overhead."

Farley leapt up. "It must be close to noon." He ran his hand through his unruly dark hair. "How could we have let this happen?"

Chloe whimpered and stood, her legs trembling.

"Sit, Chloe. Sit," Mona ordered.

"Shush, both of you. I hear something," Farley said, straining to listen.

Mona leaned against Farley listening, too.

The unmistakable patter of men could be heard close by.

Mona instinctively hunkered down as did Farley.

Chloe growled until Mona plunked her on the head. "Be quiet, Chloe. Hush."

Farley whispered, "Can you make out what they're saying?"

"I think there are two of them. They're coming this way."

"They couldn't have gotten far on foot."

Mona grabbed Farley's arm. "The horses have wandered off, and they've got them."

"I must not have secured them well enough," Farley said glumly. "My rifle was with Daisy. I've only got my pistol now."

Mona instinctively felt for her gun. "I've got mine."

"That's good. We may need them."

"We've been looking all morning."

"I've been up and down this path. There ain't no footprints."

"Then they must have gotten off the path and headed into the woods."

"If that's the case, we best be getting our tails out of here. They never saw us. They don't know who we are. Let's sell this stuff to the locals and head into Tennessee."

"I've got a set of teeth waiting for me in Jellico, but there's a body with a bullet that's got my name on it."

"Nobody can tie you to that killin'. We best be gone, Noah. We're wasting time hunting these no accounts down."

Mona jerked. "I know that voice. Robert, it's Noah, the caretaker from the Frontier Nursing Service. I remember commenting to Mary on his bad teeth."

"It makes sense. He would have known about our expedition and seen the provisions for it. Let's get ahead on the trail and confront them."

Mona grabbed Farley's arm. "No, Robert. They will fight to the bitter end. We know about Chester's death. That's an electric chair offense. They'll go down shooting rather than surrender."

"Not if we get the drop on them first. I'll go on ahead. You follow them. When I step out, you cover me from behind."

"I don't know. We can't assume there are only two of them. Maybe more." Mona felt disoriented from the lack of food. It had been over twenty-four hours since she had anything to drink or eat, and she had been in bad shape before that.

"Mona, I'm getting weak. I've been on the go for almost forty-eight hours with tracking the mules and then this. We can't hunt because they will hear the shot. It's winter, so there's nothing to forage. On foot, it's another two days to the Fugates. We need to do something."

"I'm worried that I won't be able to keep up following them."

"You've got to, Mona. We're running out of options."

"All right, Robert, but let me step out first. Just make sure they don't reach for their guns."

"Let's hurry. They're getting out of range."

Farley pulled Mona close and enveloped her in his muscular arms. "Give me a kiss for luck."

"Gladly." Mona returned Farley's kiss with such ardor it surprised them both, even though his unshaven face scratched her skin.

"It seems that you are not so weak after all," Farley kidded, patting Mona on her bottom. "When we get back to civilization, I want more kisses like that."

"You bet." She cupped his face tenderly. "When we get back, let's have a long talk about our future."

Farley spoke in the local diction. "I'd wrastle a thousand bars to hear you say that." Taking a more serious tone, he said, "We'll be okay, luv.

Don't take too long."

Mona watched Farley disappear into the forest. Quickly, she turned to Chloe. "Stay here and be still. Stay, Chloe. Stay. I'll be back for you." She covered the dog with pine branches and leaves, hoping to protect her from predators, both animal and human. With quiet determination, Mona picked up the men's trail and followed, praying Farley's plan would work.

It just had to.

Mona wasn't ready to die in the cold on a lonely mountain.

She wasn't ready to die at all.

24

Mona hurried down the path only to slip on wet leaves, ripping her pants and skinning a knee. Getting up, she spied blood on her pants where her chafed skin had bled through. She needed medical attention but couldn't think of that now. Mona had to catch up with the two men before she lost their trail. Listening for a moment, Mona couldn't hear the horses or the men speaking. "Oh God, I've lost them," she said to herself.

Tracking the hoof prints, Mona saw them lead off to the right. She stood very quietly, listening for some sound. She should have caught up with them by now. Worried, she pulled out her gun.

"Lookin' for us?" Noah said, stepping from behind an elm tree with a rifle pointed at her.

Mona trained her gun on him. "Stay where you are."

"I've got the firepower here. You drop your gun."

"Don't think I shall, if you don't mind." Mona looked about. "Where's your companion?"

"Right here," said a man inching out from behind another tree with his arm around Farley's neck and a revolver pressed against his head.

Mona flinched.

Noah said, "You might shoot me, but then Seth here will shoot your friend."

"Yes, but you'll be dead," Mona bluffed.

Farley made an attempt to cast Seth off. "Mona, shoot. Run!"

Seth knocked him down by pistol whipping him. The towering man cocked his gun aiming at Farley's face.

"Kill him, Seth. We'll keep the gurl," Noah said.

"NO!" Mona screamed. "He's worth more alive than dead. He's got lots of money."

"What's she talking about?" Seth asked, pulling up his gun.

"How does ten thousand dollars sound to you?" Mona asked.

"Ten thousand dollars?" Noah echoed, incredulously. "Where would the likes of him git so much money during the Depression?"

"We are both not who we seem. Many people would give money to get that man back safe and unharmed for ten thousand dollars. Nothing if he or I are injured."

"And who would he be?"

"He's Lawrence Robert Emerton Dagobert Farley, the Marquess of Gower. He's British nobility and in line for the British throne."

"Mona, shut up," Farley croaked, blood streaming down his face.

"You mean a redcoat? Why would someone fancy like him be traipsing in these back hills?" Noah asked.

"For a lark. An adventure," Mona replied. "If you hurt him, the British crown will hunt you down like dogs until they bring you to justice, and there will be a hanging. Your hanging."

Noah shook his head. "Don't freeze up. Shoot him, Seth."

Mona cried, "NO! No. Wait! I'll give you ten thousand dollars if you let him go and for our safe return. I've got it and lots more money."

Noah said, "How would a wee gurl have such

riches? Let's forget about her. She's worrisome. Shoot them both, Seth."

Seth uncocked his gun. "Wait a bit, Noah. I'm a-mite curious."

Mona pulled off her wool hat and then her scarf showing off her platinum hair.

Seth blustered, "She's is as pale as a haint. Look at that hair, Noah!"

"Even in these hollers, you've heard of the white-haired heiress with the yellow eyes who took over Moon Enterprises," Mona said. "We are both worth far more to you alive than dead."

"Anybody can dye their hair like Jean Harlow," Noah scoffed.

"But they can't change the color of their eyes," Mona retorted. "What do you see, Noah? Aren't my eyes the color of yellow gold?"

Noah said, "We've got our orders. You best be quiet, girlie."

"Yeah, we do all the danger and the boss gits most of the money," Seth said, angrily. "This could be our chance to git out from under."

"Hush, Seth. They know too much. Seen too much. I say we throw them off a cliff and let nature take its course." Noah waved his gun at

Mona. "You're not going to shoot me. Not with Seth ready to kill your sweetheart. That's what he is, ain't he? I don't believe a word . . ."

Seeing Noah was distracted, Mona pulled the trigger and shot him.

As soon as the shot went off, Farley grabbed Seth's feet and swept them from underneath, causing him to fall backward. His gun went off, shooting into the air, while he and Farley tussled for the firearm. Seeing the two struggle, Mona rushed over and kicked Seth in the head.

Momentarily stunned, Seth let go of the gun and Farley took hold of it.

"Well, I swanee. You shot me! You shot me!" Noah moaned. "A wee thing like yourself has bested me. Tis shame. Tis shame on me."

Mona rolled her eyes. "I got you in the shoulder. You'll live, Noah." She searched through Seth's pockets while he was still woozy from the head kick. "Look, Robert. Spanish doubloons and a five-dollar bill. I bet when we search Noah we'll find Chester's ten-dollar bill."

"That proves Rupert was telling the truth. He didn't kill Chester." Farley turned to the two scamps. "You two killed Chester Combs. These items were on him when he left base camp."

"We helped a Chester Combs up from a ravine. What happened to him after we left is none of our doin'," Noah said, nursing his bleeding shoulder. "Help me. This hurts like the dickens."

"I'm surprised you didn't kill this rascal, Mona," Farley said.

"I was aiming for his heart, but he moved at the last moment," Mona said.

"Likely story," Farley deadpanned. "Keep your gun trained on them. Here's Seth's gun. I'm going to look for the horses and the mules. The gunfire must have scared them off."

"The mules?"

"Guess who was riding them."

"I'll be here when you get back." She blew Farley a kiss while training two guns on Seth and Noah.

Farley hurried into the woods.

"Now that Lord Farley is out of the way, tell me, who is your boss?"

"What makes you think we have one?" Noah asked, tying his neck bandanna around his arm.

"Because you said so. I heard you."

"You must have heard wrong."

"No matter. The police will get the truth out of you."

"I need a doctor before I bleed to death."

"You will get some of the finest medical attention once we reach Wendover. Until then, you'll have to make do with my attention. Where's the medical kit you stole from us?"

"Don't know what you talking about."

"Suit yourself, but that kit had antiseptic, sterile bandages, and morphine. If you wish to spend hours on horseback without any painkiller to ease your way—well, my friend—that's on you. Hope you don't get blood poisoning either because the bandanna you have wrapped around your arm looks filthy."

"All right. All right. I know of a cave that Seth and I stumbled upon where some of your things might be stored."

"Stumbled upon? I see."

"Not too far from here. Go up the trail, cross the stream where two white sycamores stand as twins, turn a hard left, follow the stream until you come to a rock outcropping. Look for the entrance to a small cave. There it be."

"What will?" Farley asked, leading two horses

and two mules.

"I think where we'll find our provisions. You take these men on to the Fugates and I'll fetch the med kit. Noah needs some doctoring."

Farley shook his head. "Absolutely not. We stay together."

"They are in no shape to fight back. I'll only be an hour behind you. If I run into trouble, I shoot three times. If I'm on my way back, I'll shoot once."

"You are so plucky, it frightens me."

"If I were a man, you wouldn't think twice that my suggestion saves time."

"But you're not a man. I have to have a think on this."

"Think all you want." Mona pulled Shaggy's reins from Farley's hands and mounted Shaggy before he could react. She had learned the knack of pulling herself up. "You need medical help and so do these men. See you in an hour." She and Shaggy raced away.

Noah chuckled.

"What are you laughing about?" Farley asked.

"I'd rather face a man-eating panther than that she-cat again. You're in a world of trouble, friend, if you take her on."

"Don't I know it. Don't I know it," Farley mumbled, watching Mona disappear into the woods.

25

Mona followed Noah's directions and found the outcropping. Tying Shaggy to a tree, she searched for the cave mouth. She found it behind cut branches of pine and Kentucky cane. Throwing them aside, she crawled into the entrance with a flashlight from her saddlebag. The small entrance led to a large cavern where all the expedition's supplies were stored. She quickly located the med kit and opened it. Everything seemed intact. Rummaging around, she took a sleeping bag, stuffed a sack with oranges, apples, meat tins, sweet oats, and bottles of Ale-8-One. The liquor was gone.

It took two trips crawling in and out of the cave to load her booty upon Shaggy, but she did it while frantically eating an orange. Once loaded, she held out a hand with sweet oats for Shaggy. "I promise that I will give you all the treats you want when we are safe, Shaggy. Just stay strong for the next twelve hours. Next stop, Chloe."

It took Mona forty-five minutes to retrace her steps to find Chloe. The dog was alert and licked Mona's hands. Mona opened a bottle of Ale-8-One and let the poodle drink as much as she wanted. "Ah, you like this, huh? Drink up, girl. Drink up. Then she found a pouch of sleeping powder in the med kit and mixed some in another bottle of Ale-8-One which she coaxed Chloe to drink. "Sleep, little one. Next time you are awake, this nightmare will be over, and you'll be fit as a fiddle." Mona polished off the last bottle of the soda drink. "Gosh, that tastes good."

As Chloe drifted off, Mona stuffed her in the sleeping bag and with the last ounce of her strength, mounted Shaggy and pulled the sleeping bag off the ground and tied it around the saddle horn.

Pulling her gun from its holster, she fired one shot. Then she started down the mountain.

26

Mona never did catch up with Farley. Instead, she was met by a search party headed by Dexter Deatherage with his band of well-armed Pinkertons.

"Hello, Miss Mona."

"Hello, Dexter."

"Would you mind pointing that gun in another direction?"

"So sorry. I couldn't really see if you were friend or foe." Mona put her gun away.

"I take that it has been a rather raucous few days."

"You could say." Mona wiped her mouth. "You wouldn't have any water with you? I'm parched."

Dexter walked over to Mona still astride

Shaggy and handed her a full canteen.

Mona drank her fill and poured the rest over her face. "Ah, that feels good. Have you run into Lord Farley, by chance?"

"About three hours ago. He's been taken to the Fugates for treatment. Miss Breckinridge sent a nurse along with us. A doctor is on his way from London."

"How is Farley?"

"A bit beat up like yourself, but he'll come out okay."

"What about Noah and Seth?"

"They've been treated and are on their way to jail."

"They tried to kill us."

"So Lord Farley explained," Dexter replied in a soft voice.

Mona understood Dexter well enough to understand the nuances in his voice. "Go ahead and say it."

"Say what?"

"I told you so."

"Oh, you mean the little lecture I gave about being careful."

"Exactly."

"I don't know what you mean, Miss Mona." Dexter motioned to several Pinkertons. "Let's get you down from that horse. We have made a comfortable camp at the Fugates. You will be back in Lexington soon."

"Be careful with this sleeping bag. Chloe's inside—and my horse needs care. She's been ridden hard."

"Yes, yes, yes. Everything will be attended to. We borrowed a wagon from Wendover. Our trucks could only go so far. Got stuck in the mud."

Mona let a Pinkerton ease her off Shaggy and help her into a wagon hitched to two mules. They lay the sleeping bag next to her. Mona uncovered Chloe from the bag, relieved to find her breathing steadily. She leaned back against the wagon side and took a deep breath.

As the mules pulled the wagon, Mona spied Popcorn Pearse step out from behind a tree on the hillside and wave.

Mona did not wave back.

27

Mona was awakened to hot sloppy kisses on her face and opened one eye. "Hello, Chloe. Someone feels better this morning." She propped herself up on an elbow and petted the poodle who was beside herself with joy, her tail wagging ferociously and her body wiggling with anticipation.

"She needs to stay quiet," someone said.

Startled, Mona turned her head. "Althea! When did you get in?"

"Your men came and found me, escorted me back to Wendover, and here I am. I got in sometime before you arrived, but you were asleep in the wagon. I had to attend to other duties."

Mona sat up, rubbing the sleep from her eyes. "I admit I was running on fumes. I was supposed to be in Lexington yesterday, but they held my transport up. Made me stay another night. You know why?"

"Something to do with Noah and Seth I think. The doctor from London bandaged their wounds, Mary fed them, and your men sent them on their merry way to the Leslie County jail. Apparently something happened after they were incarcerated. Both became ill. Noah is dead and Seth is at death's door."

"You said they became ill after they arrived at the Leslie County jail?"

"That's what it looks like. What? Do you think someone at the jail did something to them?"

Mona slowly scooted out of bed and searched her nightstand drawer. "I guess it was to appear so."

"Well, whatever, there's a big brouhaha about it. Never mind about that. I came to give you a tonic. It's my own concoction from nature's plants. Will help you get back on your feet lickety-split. I hope you don't mind me saying so, but you look awful, Mona. Your color is off, and you're covered with bruises and cuts." Althea looked about. "If you have makeup, I can cover the bruises with it."

Ignoring Althea, Mona kept searching the room.

Confused at Mona's actions, Althea tried another tactic, "After you take the tonic, I'll help you wash your hair. It badly needs it."

"Leave the glass on the table. I'll take the tonic in a moment." Mona looked in the dresser drawers and then spied her saddlebag in a chair.

"I'd feel better if you would take it now."

Mona sat in the chair rummaging through the knapsack. "I'll drink it. I promise. Put it on the table over there."

"Be a doll and take it now. Hmm?" Irritated that Mona was not paying attention, Althea advanced toward Mona and snapped, "Whatever are you searching for?"

"This," Mona said. Not finding her gun, Mona picked up the fireplace poker and brandished it. "Althea, stand away from me."

Althea gasped. "What are you doing? Point that thing away from me."

"It's going to stay right where it is. Have you given this concoction to Bob Farley?"

"No. He went with your lawyer, Dexter Deatherage, to Leslie County to see about Noah and Seth. He recovered quicker than you and has been up for hours."

"But he wouldn't have been a target anyway because he didn't see the location of the cave. I did."

"Mona, please. You're frightening me. What cave are you talking about?"

"Noah and Seth talked about having a boss. I figure that must be you."

"Have you gone out of your senses? I've never heard such rot. I'm going to call the doctor."

"You may leave but put that glass down. What's in it, Althea? A little bit of foxglove? Nightshade maybe. Dexter said a nurse was being sent up. Were you the nurse sent with Deatherage to the Fugates? Did you give Noah and Seth the same tonic when fixing them up for the trip to the county jail? Perhaps telling them it was a pick-me-up with a little whiskey in it? They trusted you, didn't they? I would guess it was something slow acting so the authorities couldn't tie it to you. You couldn't afford for them to talk. You must have circled back to Wendover. How did you explain to Mary that you left us?"

"My horse became lame. I had to return. I don't know how you can believe Noah over me."

Mona scoffed. "Noah couldn't find the prize in a Cracker Jack box if his life depended on it, let alone mastermind months of theft up and down the mountain ridge."

"You should be looking at Popcorn Pearse."

"I thought about him, but he said someone was messing around with his still. I think he was following us because he thought it would lead him to the culprit. And there was another thing. You said you knew where all the stills were on the mountain, but yet, you were startled when Pearse confronted us on the road that second day. I think he suspected you, Althea, and was sending you a message."

"No one will believe you, Mona. You've had a bad shock. Let me help you." Althea stepped toward Mona.

Mona raised the poker as if to strike. "If you are innocent, leave the glass on the table and walk out. If it tests negative for poison, I will apologize, followed up with a nice fat check to appease your sense of outrage."

Grinning, Althea tipped the glass down and poured the liquid out onto the floor.

Mona leaned back in her chair. "It makes sense. Rose Fugate said someone was stealing valuable horses, mules, and livestock up and down Pine Mountain. Who but a FNS nurse would know who had what? You made your rounds, saw what people had, and then gave Noah orders to filch the merchandise. Noah would then take the stolen goods and sell them in Tennessee. We're not too far from the state border, are we?"

Althea didn't reply but cast her eyes about the room looking for some sort of escape.

"I suspect you were the nurse who helped the doctor examine Noah and Seth. You poisoned those men with your knowledge of mountain herbal medicine. You're an expert on which plants heal and which plants destroy. You killed those men just as you are trying to kill me with your tonic."

"You can't prove any of this."

Mona shook her head. "No, I can't, but I would surmise that Farley and Dexter Deatherage went to the jail for a deathbed confession.

There's the possibility that Seth is spilling his guts right now."

"I doubt it. There was a muscle constrictor in the solution, you see. It would have been impossible for them to speak."

"Lovely," Mona sneered. "Something similar to the symptoms of lockjaw. I need to ask one question before you take your leave of me. Why?"

"I needed money to finish my education."

"You stole from the people you came here to help!"

"Think about how much more I could help if I was a doctor. I could open a clinic. Then these people could get real help."

"You made your patients suffer. These people's lives are harsh enough but without their animals, life is intolerable."

"I'm not going to be lectured by the likes of you. You have everything you want at your fingertips. You have no idea what it's like to be poor and struggle."

"Oh, don't I?" Mona said. "You make me sick, Althea. Go on. Get out of here. Take one of the cars and take off. Get as far away as you can from me and Mary Breckinridge and the other fine nurses you have besmirched."

Althea hesitated for a moment. "I'll be taking this glass with me. Don't want to leave any incriminating evidence behind."

"Get out!" Mona yelled. "Get away from me!"

Althea backed out of the room and fled.

Mona immediately sopped up the wetness on the floor with a pillowcase. Then she ran outside and stopped on the porch, observing Althea drive off. "Darn. I was hoping I could prevent her from leaving."

A Pinkerton man standing guard said, "Miss Althea said you gave her permission to take one of the cars." If he was surprised that Mona was standing before him with her hair in disarray and in her nightgown without the benefit of a robe or slippers, he didn't betray it.

Mona watched until Althea was out of sight. "Did you note the car she took? Take down the license plate number?"

"Yes, ma'am."

"Did she take a dog with her?"

"Yes, ma'am. Was she not supposed to?"

"I was curious."

"Yes, ma'am."

"I have an article I wish taken to a lab in Lexington."

"Yes, ma'am."

"Number one priority. Understand? I want the results today. I don't care what it costs."

"Yes, ma'am. Will you be leaving for Lexington yourself, Miss Mona?"

"I'll be staying for a couple more days. I have some things to tie up here. One more thing. Call the sheriff. I have something to tell him."

"Very good, ma'am." The Pinkerton motioned to a man stationed at the foot of the drive.

The young private detective came running.

"Miss Mona has something she wants you to do."

The detective looked expectantly at Mona. "Yes?"

"Are you a good driver?" she asked.

"Yes, ma'am. I am."

"Can you drive fast?"

"If need be."

"Then follow me. I have an article I want you to take to a lab in Lexington."

The junior detective shot a look at his superior while following Mona into the house.

His superior shrugged. After all, it was not his place to question their boss. If Mona Moon wanted to run around in her nighty, so be it. He just wanted to receive his paycheck each week. The Pinkerton sighed and closed the door after them. All was well and right with the world as far as he was concerned.

28

"What are you going to do with all this stuff?" Farley asked, several days later. He watched men carrying the expedition's supplies to wagons outside the cave.

"I'll have the men take it to Mary Breckenridge. She can dispense the food and the tools to whomever she sees fit. We have no need of it anymore."

"What are you going to do about Althea?"

"I don't know. I can't prove anything. The pillowcase revealed nothing. It was too compromised for the lab technicians to find anything. At least, nothing in the quantity that we needed to prove Althea as a murderer."

"The autopsies of Noah and Seth proved they were poisoned."

"But it doesn't prove that Althea poisoned them. She can claim the doctor did it or someone at the jail slipped them something. There's just not enough evidence."

"What about her confession to you?"

Mona tossed her head. "She said. I said. She can claim I was overwrought from my experience. Dehydrated—that type of thing. Imagined the whole conversation. Blab. Blab. Blab. You know how it would go in court."

"I guess it doesn't matter anyway. We can't find her."

"Exactly."

"That leaves Rupert Hunt or whatever his name is. What are you going to do about him?"

"I hired him."

"YOU WHAT!"

"I hired the man, my darling. I had Dexter ferret Rupert out and hire him. His real name is Reginald Baxter."

"But whatever for?"

"Because it takes a thief to catch a thief. He is going undercover in my company to ferret out embezzlers, thieves, and other forms of corruption. I've sent him to our copper mines out west.

There seem to be some miscalculations in the books."

"He'll steal you blind, Mona."

"It's the perfect solution, Robert. Rupert is not a violent man and is incredibly intelligent. Besides, he's sneaky. He fooled us, didn't he?"

Farley looked away.

"Well, didn't he?"

"Yes," Farley said, begrudgingly. "But my saucy cow, he kidnapped you."

"And it was genius. Kidnapping a person who doesn't know they are being kidnapped. Yes, it was pure genius. So you see, he's perfect to go undercover. I am paying Rupert very well, and he gets a cut of every theft he recovers. He'll work very hard for me as long as I keep dangling that money carrot. Besides, he liked Chloe. That makes him square with me."

"What about his conspirator?"

"Dexter didn't pay the ransom, so we never knew who his friend was. Oh, it's such a bother."

"That you didn't discover Rupert's friend?"

"No. That Dexter was right. I should have listened. I put everyone in danger."

"Marry me. I'll protect you."

"Stay sober for a year and ask me then."

"Would you get off that high horse?"

"I'm worth waiting for, Robert. Show me that you can stay off the bottle and give me the engagement ring that I want. I happened to be in a jewelry store last month and saw one that I liked very much."

Farley pulled Mona closed and nuzzled her neck. "You little vixen. You had planned to marry me all along. You just wanted to make me suffer."

Laughing, Mona pushed Farley. "Hush now. The workers." She pointed at the men rushing about them hauling items out of the cave.

"I don't give a tinker's damn about them," Farley growled.

"Stay sober, Robert. I'm basing my future happiness on you."

A worker scurried out with the last box from the cave. Mona and Robert heard the wagons and mules start for Wendover.

"We're alone now. Let's neck," Farley suggested, wagging his eyebrows.

"There's something I need to show you." Mona moved to the back of the cave with her flashlight.

"What now?" Farley asked, exasperated. "We get a moment to ourselves, and you want to show me something that doesn't deal with you undressing."

"Robert, come look at this," Mona insisted. She flashed a light upon the wall.

The initials JS were incised on the wall of the cave. Four other sets of initials accompanied them along with the date of 1764.

"And this, too," Mona said excitedly. She pulled silver English crowns from her pocket. "I found these over there in the dirt."

Farley took the crowns and studied the dates. "1763 dated on this one." He turned over another one. "This one says 1762." He looked up astonished. "Mona, do you know what this means? You have discovered John Swift's mine. You've done it!"

"I think so. Can you believe it?" Mona laughed while Farley did a little jig.

"What are you going to do about it? This will be quite a feather in your cap."

"We're not going to tell anyone. In fact, as soon as the wagons are far enough away, you are going to seal the entrance."

"With what, my dear?"

"I instructed my men to leave two sticks of dynamite by the mouth of the cave. I will take the horses down the mountain to a safe distance and wait for you. Here is a book of matches."

"But why, Mona? People have been looking for this mine since 1769."

"Because I think it is cursed. What if Swift really did kill all his men to hide the locations of the mine? The silver would be steeped in blood. I want to be away from the mine and all the heartache that goes with it. It will bring nothing but trouble."

Farley reluctantly took the box of matches. "All right then. Take the horses and go down the hill. I'll follow shortly."

Mona kissed Farley and took her leave, taking Shaggy and Daisy to a safe distance down the mountain.

They tried to bolt when they heard the explosion echo off the walls of the mountains, but Mona held onto them, speaking calmly to them. The horses quieted down and were grazing near the pathway when Farley joined Mona after an hour or so.

"I cut tree branches and piled around the entrance as well, but someone will eventually find it, Mona, and remove the rubble. Perhaps though, we will be old and gray by that time and not give a hoot."

"Perhaps," Mona replied.

Farley gathered the horses and helped Mona onto Shaggy before he mounted Daisy.

As Mona and Farley headed down the mountain, they ran into three men. They stopped and chatted with the men for a moment, discovering that they were transporting a new cast iron cook stove addressed to Rosamond Flora Fugate.

Farley noticed the crate had a Mooncrest Enterprise label on it. He beamed a smile at Mona. "That's decent of you, I must say."

"Come on, boy of mine. Let these men do their work." She urged Shaggy forward humming a tune she had learned from Rose—Barbara Allen.

I tried to get the cadence and the speech of the Appalachian people in 1933 as authentic as I could. Since my mother was Appalachian many expressions used in this story were second nature to me. However, the Appalachian Mountains are vast, and people speak differently in diverse parts of the mountain range. I did the best I could with their spoken language.

The history has been researched and is accurate based on the information read. Hopefully, I will be forgiven if something is amiss. Read on for more information.

Ale-8-One

A ginger-based soft drink developed by G. L. Wainscott in Winchester, Kentucky during the Roaring Twenties. It is still in production.

Autobahn

The autobahn formed the first straight, high-speed road network in the world. The first section of the highway from Frankfurt to Darmstadt opened in 1935. Adolph Hitler appointed Fritz Todt as the Inspector General of the German Road Construction, and by 1936, 130,000 were working directly on autobahn construction in the rest of the country and another 270,000 workers were supplying items needed for the construction. During WWII, the median strips were paved over to allow airplanes to land.

Impressed with the autobahn system, President Eisenhower signed the Federal Highway Act of 1956 to eliminate unsafe roads, inefficient routes, and all things that got in the way of "speedy, safe transcontinental travel." The highways were also designed to promote quick transport of troops if the need arose since the railroads had diminished in importance.

Barbara Allen
Scottish love ballad from the 1600s.

Black Dog
English term for depression and its use is associated with Winston Churchill.

Blue Fugates
The Fugates were a family who lived in Eastern Kentucky and known as the "Blue Fugates" because their skin was tinted blue because of a recessive gene. Martin Fugate married Elizabeth Smith who were both carriers of the genetic trait which created methemoglobinemia. This causes blue skin. Many of their descendants carried this gene and were not cured until the mid-twentieth century, when they were treated with methylene blue by nurse Ruth Pendergrass and hematologist Madison Cawein III who published his findings in 1964.

Charles and Anne Lindbergh

Twenty-month-old son of famous aviator Charles Lindbergh and Anne Morrow Lindbergh was kidnapped from his crib on March 1, 1932. In May, the child's body was discovered by the side of a nearby road. Richard Hauptmann was arrested, found guilty, and executed for the crime. Congress passed the Federal Kidnapping Act (also called the Lindbergh Law) which made transporting a kidnapped victim across state lines a federal crime. Charles Lindbergh flew the first solo, nonstop transatlantic flight from New York to Paris. His plane, Spirit of St. Louis, is considered one of the most famous planes in the world and is on display at the National Air and Space Museum in Washington, D.C.

Coca-Cola

In 1885, Confederate Colonel John Pemberton needed to find an alternative for his morphine addiction due to a wound suffered during the Civil War. In the formula for his new drink, Pemberton added cocaine from the coca leaf and caffeine from the African kola nut, thus the name—Coca-Cola. In 1886, it was sold as a health tonic at drug store fountains where carbonated water was added. The formula was sold to Asa Candler, who formed the Coca-Cola Company in 1892. Plans to bottle Coca-Cola were introduced in 1899, and the drink's popularity grew with the Temperance Movement and Prohibition. Public pressure made the company remove cocaine from its formula in 1929.

Duncan Hines
(1880-1959)

Born in Bowling Green, Kentucky, Duncan Hines was a pioneer of restaurant and hotel ratings for travelers. As a traveling salesman, he made a list of good restaurants in which to eat because health codes were not uniform across the country, and food poisoning was common. The list was so popular Hines published books and became a household name. In 1953, Hines sold his name and titles of a few of his books to the Hines-Park Foods. Later, Hines' rights were sold to Procter and Gamble in 1957. Cake mixes still proudly display his name in the grocery store.

1935 – *Adventures in Good Eating*

1938 – *Lodging for a Night*

1955 – *The Duncan Hines Barbecue Cook Book*

1955 – *The Duncan Hines Dessert Book*

El Dorado
Europeans, during the 16th and 17th centuries, searched for a mythical city made of gold in the New World.

Frontier Nursing Service
Founded by Mary Breckinridge in 1925, the Frontier Nursing Service was to provide health care for women and children in remote areas of Kentucky. The organization was first known as the Kentucky Committee for Mothers and Babies. Midwives traveled into the mountains on horseback and mules. The organization is still in existence but now associated with other health care systems.

Hernando de Soto
(1500-1542)
Spanish conquistador best known for exploring the southern United States and being the first European to cross the Mississippi River.

Hobo Nickels
Buffalo nickels were re-sculpted by bored men crisscrossing America looking for work during the Great Depression. These men were known

for riding the railways illegally and were referred to as "hobos."

Indians
The term "Indian" was used to describe indigenousness peoples from North American prior to 1960. The terms "Native Americans" or "First Nations" did not come into common use until after the mid-twentieth century. It is not my intention to be disrespectful, but to use a word customarily applied to describe native peoples of the Americas by those of European descent in the 1930s.

James Harrod
(1746-1792)
Harrod was a renowned longhunter, soldier, pioneer, explorer, and contemporary of Daniel Boone and Simon Kenton. In 1774, he founded the first permanent settlement in Kentucky known as Harrodstown, later renamed Harrodsburg. He disappeared on a "hunting trip." It is thought by many that he was looking for John Swift's mine and was murdered.

John Swift

Folklore of the Appalachian Mountains. A John Swift mined a Native American silver mine or mines in an undisclosed location(s) from 1761 to 1769. Mine(s) could not be relocated as Swift went blind.

Longhunter

Eighteenth-century European explorers/hunters who would gather into parties of two or four men and traveled to Southwest Virginia (included Kentucky, West Virginia, and Tennessee). They would hunt from October until April and return home. This type of hunting occurred only at this period in history and in this area. It did not expand further west. Daniel Boone was one such man who went on a "long hunt" for years before returning home.

Poodles

There is confusion about who first bred the poodle designed to hunt fowl. Some say the Germans. Others say the poodle descended from the French Barbet. Regardless, this highly intelligent dog became a favorite with royal courts. German artist, Albrecht Durer, drew the dog in the 15th century. As a breed, the poodle has been around a long time.

Pack Horse Library Project

Illiteracy in Eastern Kentucky was thirty-one percent in the first half of the twentieth century. Sixty-three Kentucky counties had no library services, so the Pack Horse Library Project was born. The Kentucky Federation of Women's Clubs began the first traveling library program in 1896 and ended it in 1933. One year later, one of President Roosevelt's programs, the Federal Emergency Relief Administration started the program again. It was then handed off to the WPA who hired "book ladies" at $28 per month to ride upon horses and mules, delivering donated books to private homes and organizations. The project ended in 1943.

Pine Mountain

Pine Mountain is a ridge in the Appalachian Mountains running through Kentucky, Tennessee, and Virginia.

Pine Mountain Settlement

Founded in 1913 as a school for children in

Southeastern Kentucky. William Creech donated land and recruited Katherine Pettit and Ethel DeLong to establish the school. Creech was concerned by the lack of education in the area where there were many social problems and lack of medical care. The school boarded students because transportation was poor due to lack of roads and became the headquarters for the Pack Horse Library Project. Today, the school focuses on environmental education.

Swanee
Slang for "swear."

You're not done yet!

Read On For Exciting Bonus Chapters

MURDER UNDER A WOLF MOON

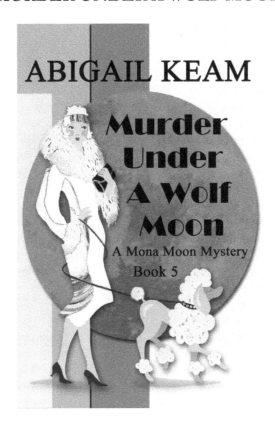

ABIGAIL KEAM

Murder Under A Wolf Moon

A Mona Moon Mystery

Book 5

1

"You look crackers tonight, darling," Lord Farley said to Mona as they sped along Versailles Road at twenty-five miles per hour in Mona's chauffeur-driven red and black Daimler. It was dark and the road was slippery with ice.

Mona smiled and answered, "Thank you, Robert. A lady always likes to be complimented, but in America the word 'crackers' has a negative connotation."

Robert replied, "Then you look ravishing. How's that?"

Mona nodded and took a sterling compact out of her purse in order to check her lipstick.

Robert gave Mona the once-over. She was wearing her sleeveless black velvet gown with the sweetheart neckline and elbow-length black gloves. The dress was accented by a long strand of pearls held together by a diamond clip. Her evening coat was a heavy, black brocade as the night was cold due to a winter storm several days before.

Mona glanced over at Robert, approving of his evening tux, black cape, and silver-handled walking stick. He also smelled divine. "You look mighty spiffy yourself."

"Spiffy. That's a new American term for me."

"It means you look okay, bub."

"Darling! You're shivering."

"I'm cold. I think I'm still recovering from our trek to the mountains."

"It was a shame you missed your first Christmas and New Year's Eve in Moon Manor only to be fighting for your life on Pine Mountain."

"I was bored and wanted some adventure," Mona laughed. "That's what I got—only the joke was played on me."

"A little too much adventure."

Mona placed her hand over Robert's. "The only thing I regret is that I put you in danger. I can never forgive myself for doing so. I should have checked out Rupert Hunt more thoroughly.

I'm so sorry, Robert. Really."

"I never liked the man, but I must say his scheme to kidnap you without you knowing it was devilishly clever. He got you to go along with his plan willingly."

"So you forgive me for hiring Rupert later?"

"I guess it takes a thief to catch a thief."

"He's already given Moon Enterprises good information on embezzling in our Butte, Montana office."

"Hiring him is not something I would have done, but things seem to have a way of working out for you, Mona."

"Yes, it's a brand new year and all that trouble is behind us. Roosevelt is fixing the country, and we are heading toward a brighter future."

Robert kissed the inside of Mona's wrist. "And our future as well."

Mona looked deeply into Robert's eyes. "To our future as well," she echoed before shivering again.

"Why aren't you wearing one of your grandmother's fur coats?"

"I hate wearing dead animal skins. It makes me feel—well, uneasy."

Lawrence Robert Emerton Dagobert Farley, Marquess of Gower, had noticed that Mona was slowly weeding her wardrobe of leather and furs. He had thought this new indulgence odd, but had said nothing. Instead, Robert was rather proud of Mona's compassion for animals. Pulling her close, he said, "Let me warm you. It is a chilly night."

Mona snuggled close to him, sighing contentedly.

"I see you are still not wearing my engagement ring."

"I shall wear it when we announce our betrothal and not before."

"Let's do it tonight."

"And spoil the evening for our hostess? I should say not. By the way, who exactly are our host and hostess tonight?"

Robert pulled out a linen paper invitation from his pocket. "Mr. and Mrs. Cornelius Vanderbilt Hopper."

"The Vanderbilt family?"

"A minor cousin with the name but none of the money. Cornelius goes by the name of Connie."

"Did you know that a centurion named Cornelius was directed by an angel to contact St. Peter? After he spoke with Peter, he converted to Christianity and is considered the first gentile convert. Here's another fun fact, Connie means wolf in old German."

"You know the oddest trivia."

Mona shrugged. "I guess I thought of it because there is a wolf moon tonight."

"A what?"

"A full moon in January is called a wolf moon. Don't ask me why. It just is."

Robert peered out of the car window at the sky. "It is a full moon. I didn't even notice. Looks like it's going to snow, too." He leaned back in the seat and put his arm around Mona.

"What else can you tell me about them?" Mona asked.

"The family did have money at one time, but Connie's father was a notorious gambler and frittered all the family's money away."

"Ooh, not good."

"I mean they are not poor by any means, but the family is not Vanderbilt rich anymore. They are just comfortable." Robert thought for a moment. "Well, maybe scratching by. I've heard tales."

"They can't be too poor if they are throwing a big shindig tonight. Champagne costs money."

"Connie is throwing this bash for everyone to meet his new young wife. She has some money, which is why he can afford this bash."

"Go on."

"Her name is Elspeth Neferet Alden. Her father was Sir Jonathon Alden."

"The famous Egyptologist?"

"I knew that would impress you."

"Oh, my goodness. I can't wait to meet her and talk about her father's exploits."

Robert was delighted when Mona's yellow eyes lit up with excitement. She liked nothing better than to discuss the ancient world in the Near East. It was her passion.

The Daimler pulled up in front of a beige limestone mansion with its windows blazing with light as though a thousand candles had been lit. Jamison, Mona's chauffeur, opened the car door.

Robert jumped out first and gave a hand to Mona, who stared at the mansion.

Mona commented, "This is bigger than Moon

Mansion. Must cost a fortune for the upkeep."

"Now you see the need for this marriage."

"Oh," was all Mona could utter before the door was opened by the butler and Mona was whisked out of the cold.

2

Mona handed her wrap to a maid and then let Robert escort her into the ballroom. A live orchestra was playing the latest popular radio tunes, and the floor was alive with guests dancing the foxtrot, while older couples danced the black bottom and Charleston.

Robert and Mona stood in the receiving line and waited their turn to greet their hosts. Finally, Mona was presented to Cornelius Vanderbilt Hopper.

"It's a pleasure meeting you," Cornelius said. He kissed Mona's hand. "Everything they say about you is true. You are a beauty like the rarest orchid."

"Not half of what *they* say about me is accurate Mr. Hopper," Mona replied. She didn't know what to make of Hopper's flamboyant comments.

"I thought people were exaggerating about your hair, but it is truly platinum, without any benefit of color—and your eyes—a true yellow, more of a golden hue I would think."

Annoyed, Robert stepped in and held out his hand. "Good to see you again, Connie."

Shaking his hand, Hopper said, "Robert, how nice to see you. Are you here with this gorgeous creature?"

"Yes, I am, so mittens off."

"Speaking of gorgeous creatures, may I present my wife, Elspeth Neferet Alden Hopper."

Both Robert and Mona turned to the petite, dusky-skinned, dark-haired woman with black soulful eyes standing beside Hopper. Robert gave a little bow, but Mona was so smitten with admiration that she could barely find words to speak.

Mrs. Hopper was wearing a pleated, linen sheath adorned with a large Egyptian collar called a wesekh made of gold, turquoise, coral, onyx, and lapis lazuli. The woman's dark eyes were outlined in kohl like the ancient Egyptians. The only difference in her makeup from that of an ancient woman was that Mrs. Hopper wore bright red lipstick.

For a second, Mona thought she was addressing Nefertiti. "Em hotep."

Mrs. Hopper became animated and said, "Ii-wey. You speak ancient Egyptian?"

"Just a few lines I picked up when I was in Cairo. I am more familiar with Sumerian and Babylonian words. I must say I am so taken with your collar. It looks authentic."

"My father made it from bits and pieces he found in the sand. He presented it to me on my eighteenth birthday."

"Lucky girl," Mona said, barely taking her eyes off the collar. Jewelry was a weakness of Mona's.

"My dear, people are waiting," Connie said to Elspeth.

"You're right, Connie. Forgive me. Miss Moon, I hope we have a chance to speak again this evening."

Mona said, "Please, we must. I am dying to talk about the Near East and your adventures excavating Queen Ahsetsedek's tomb."

Elspeth asked, "You know of my father's work?"

"Who doesn't know about John Alden and his famous find in the Valley of the Queens?" Mona said.

"Dear!" Connie said as though annoyed.

For a second, Elspeth's eyes dampened but she nodded and smiled.

Robert led Mona over to a chair. "Happy?"

"I'm ecstatic, Robert. I'm so glad you made me come. Think of it—John Alden's daughter. Oh, the stories she must have. I can't wait to get her alone."

"Are you up for a dance while you're waiting?"

"Assuredly."

Robert led Mona onto the dance floor where they did the foxtrot, a waltz, and another foxtrot until Mona begged off.

"It's hot in this room, that's for sure," Robert said.

"I need to freshen up. Can you excuse me?"

"Don't take too long. I see some captains of industry heading my way for some boring shop talk."

"I promise."

Mona gathered her clutch from the coat check

maid and headed for the downstairs bathroom for the ladies, but it was too crowded, so she asked if she could use the upstairs one. The maid pointed to a powder room on the second floor. Mona quickly bounded up the grand staircase and headed down a carpeted hallway. Passing one of the doors cracked open, she heard crying—a deep mournful crying. Standing at the door, Mona looked both ways, wondering what she should do. No one else was in the hallway. Crying was a private act and Mona didn't want to intrude, but crying also meant someone might need help. She knocked on the door and peeked in. Inside a spacious and luxurious bedroom, Elspeth sat on a chair holding her magnificent necklace.

"Elspeth, what is the matter?" Mona quickly closed the door, locked it, and went to the weeping bride.

"You shouldn't be in here."

"You shouldn't be crying at your own party." Mona dragged a chair close to Elspeth. "Now tell me. What is the matter?"

"Connie told me to change into something more conservative. He said my dress embarrassed him and looked like something a person would wear at Halloween."

"You looked stunning. I love the collar. In fact, I have half a mind to steal it," Mona teased.

Elspeth looked at Mona through thick, tear-stained eyelashes. "I wore it to honor my father. Did you really like my outfit?"

"My dear, your dress was fascinating and quite wonderful. Who cares what Connie says?"

"I don't want to make my husband angry."

"Okay, change then, but no more tears. Don't let those people downstairs see you cry, and when you go back down, tell everyone you tore the hem of your linen dress while dancing." Mona went over to a wall, which was lined with mirrors. "Is this your closet?"

Elspeth nodded.

Mona threw open all the mirrored doors to Elspeth's wardrobe. "Let's find the most seductive gown you have."

"Connie wants me to wear something conservative."

"Listen, my dear, if you give in to ridiculous demands now, your husband won't give you a moment's peace. You will never be your own woman. Understand?"

Elspeth wiped away a tear. "It's true what they say about you."

"What's that?" Mona asked, rummaging through the closet.

"That you are different. A leopard among house cats."

"Do they? That's rather nice, don't you think? I like leopards. I recently had a bout with a mountain panther."

"Who won?"

Mona laughed. "It was a draw." She pulled a low-cut red chiffon dress from the closet. "This will do nicely. Wear this."

"Oh, no. I can't. It's too risqué."

"You'll wear it or you'll be under your husband's thumb the rest of your life. Now, we need some jewelry. Do you have a necklace to set off that dress?"

"I have a diamond choker."

"Do you have something that will plunge into your cleavage?"

Elspeth's hands fluttered a bit. "I have a ruby and diamond pin that can change into a necklace."

"Sounds perfect." Mona threw the dress at Elspeth. "Put it on." She went over to Elspeth's vanity and rummaged through her jewelry box finding the pin and then a heavy chain for it. Mona clasped the necklace around Elspeth neck. "Looks lovely. Now we need to fix your makeup." Mona dusted Elspeth's face with powder and redid her lipstick with a brighter shade of red.

"I hope Connie likes this dress."

"He probably won't. He'll make a fuss after the party."

"I don't want that."

"It doesn't matter what dress you select. He will deem it inappropriate. Don't you under-stand?"

"What do you mean?"

Mona looked Elspeth directly in the eyes. "You know exactly what I mean." She grabbed one of Elspeth's arms. "Where did you get that bruise?"

Elspeth pulled her arm away. "I fell."

"Sure you did."

"It was an accident."

"Sure it was."

Elspeth looked away. "I have no friends or family here. It's terribly frightening being alone in a strange place without anyone to talk with."

"Then you must come to tea tomorrow at Moon Manor. I know what it is like to be alone in new surroundings. Tell Connie I'm having a hen party so you can meet more ladies in the community. Will you come?"

"That's awfully sweet of you, but you needn't bother with me. We don't know each other and—I don't want to be a nuisance."

"I have tea at four o'clock. Be there."

"Will you walk down with me? I don't want to face Connie in this dress alone."

"Of course. I need to use the powder room first though. Nature calls." Mona strode off to the bathroom and after refreshing herself, checking her outfit, and putting on more lipstick, she entered Elspeth's bedroom only to find her gone.

"She left without me," Mona said to herself. She hurried to the grand staircase where she discovered Connie berating Elspeth on the stair landing. Elspeth was looking down at her feet and anxiously twisting a handkerchief between two sweaty palms.

"My goodness," Mona called out from above. "You've changed into another dress, Elspeth." She hurried down the steps and twirled Elspeth around. "It's a stunner, dear. Don't you think so, Mr. Hopper, I mean, Connie?" Mona didn't give him time to answer. "Come on, Elspeth. You'll simply bowl people over. I know a lot of women here tonight who will want a gander at your necklace. Ruby, isn't it? From India? Two stunning necklaces in one night. You put us all to shame."

Mona turned to Connie. "You must be so proud. Your wife is surely going to be the social butterfly of the season. Come Elspeth. You must show this dress off. Will you excuse us, Connie— or would you like the honor of escorting your wife?"

Connie's face flushed red and was so overcome with anger, he couldn't sputter any reply to Mona, nor would he have if he could have found the words. He realized she was toying with him, so all he could do was to take his wife's arm and guide her down the stairs into the ballroom. Connie wouldn't dare offend Mona, as she was too powerful.

"Don't forget tea tomorrow at four, Elspeth. Ladies only. I insist," Mona called after her. Smiling, Mona glided down the staircase into the arms of Robert.

Robert asked, "Why do you look so pleased with yourself?"

"I just bullied a bully."

"Really?"

"Yes, really."

"Tell me about it in the car. Ready to skip this popsicle stand?"

"Most assuredly."

"I'll grab our coats. You say goodbye to our hosts."

Mona shook her head. "I really think we can forget that part of the evening."

Robert laughed. "What did you do, darling?"

"I'll tell you about it at your house in front of a roaring fire with hot chocolate."

"Will you stay the night?"

"And give the servants something to gossip about? No way, but I might be convinced to see the wolf moon sink behind the horizon."

"I'll take what I can get." Robert rushed off to gather their coats. With the promise of a little snogging, Robert couldn't wait to get Mona to his house. And there was Mona's encounter. Robert could only guess what had occurred.

Hmm—what could Mona possibly have instigated now?

3

Robert was nibbling Mona's earlobe.

"What can you tell me about Connie Hopper?" she asked.

"How can you think about Connie when I'm doing this?" Robert nuzzled Mona's neck.

"Feels lovely."

"More the response I was hoping for, woman. Now turn around so I can give you a proper snog. Let's swap some saliva."

After kissing for a while, Mona came up for air. "How well do you know Hopper?"

"You still thinking about that man? If you are going to think about another man while I'm trying to seduce you, what chance do we have?"

"Don't sulk, Robert. You know how my mind works. There's a puzzle concerning Espeth and

Connie. My mind can't turn off. It keeps racing."

Robert reached for a cigarette and lit it.

"I wish you wouldn't smoke, Robert."

"I smoke out of frustration, Mona. It's due to you."

"The sooner you tell me the sooner we can get back to necking."

"Oh, well, then." Robert stubbed out his cigarette and took a sip of his coffee while Mona took a drink of her hot chocolate spiked with a touch of liqueur. He didn't know how she could stand the combination. Robert did know that he couldn't touch liquor for a year in order to get Mona to marry him. He also knew Mona deliberately tempted him by drinking alcohol in front of him. She was a devil. "I don't know him very well. He's quite a bit older than I. We're not in business or anything like that."

"How do you know him?"

"I guess the Bluegrass social circuit. Love of horse racing, that sort of thing."

"What do people say about him?"

Robert shrugged. "Not much, I'm afraid. Connie's always been very low key. No scandals of any sort. He has reasonably good manners.

Knows which fork to use at a dinner party and never discusses politics or religion with anyone. Never gossips about anyone. Never been seen in the female servants' quarters after midnight. He's one dull boy if you ask me."

"Unlike you."

"Definitely unlike me."

"Hmm."

"Why this interest in Connie Hopper? Did he do something to you? Shall I fight him in a duel at dawn?"

"I was just wondering."

"Wondering what?"

"Why a young woman like Elspeth, who is British and has her own money, would marry a much older man who is American and basically broke?"

"You once called the British snobs of the worst kind."

"I did?"

"Yes, you did and you're quite right. Elspeth doesn't have the right breeding credentials for a brilliant upper class British marriage."

Mona looked flummoxed. "She's John Alden's daughter, the greatest Egyptologist who ever lived. He discovered Queen Ahsetsedek IV's tomb intact."

"John Alden was born in an East London slum from an unmarried working girl, if you know what I mean."

"I see where this is going. I guess it doesn't matter that Alden elevated himself from the 'gutter' and worked his way to a Ph.D. from Oxford."

"I never mentioned the word gutter."

"But that's what you meant."

"I'm trying to tell you why Elspeth married whom she did if you let me finish."

"Sorry."

"John Alden was a cockney who went on to achieve many wonderful things, but then he marries an Egyptian native, which resulted in Elspeth."

"I see what you're saying. The noses of the blue bloods across the pond were bent out of shape, and they wouldn't let Elspeth play with their sons."

"Exactly. Both classism and racism played into the scenario."

"Well, boy of mine. What are *they* going to say

about me when we marry?"

"My British *friends* are going to insult you behind your back, but they will be polite to your face. You're too rich for them to offend, and they can't afford to be rude because they figure that in twenty years they'll palm one of their worthless offspring onto one of our offspring. That's the way it will be."

"Why should I marry you?"

"Because you love me and no matter what, we are going to do what we want to do—similar to what your parents did. They crossed social lines to be married, didn't they?"

"Oh, how can I refuse you, Robert, when you make such sense? Yes, my father lost the Moon inheritance because he married my mother."

"Were they happy, Babycakes?"

"They loved each other very much. It hurt my father to lose his inheritance, but he loved my mother too much to let her go. Yes, Robert, they were fortunate because they realized money can't bring happiness. Love does."

"Money can sure keep wolves away from the door, though," Robert teased. On a more serious note, he said, "We'll be okay, Mona. Trust me.

No one will ever hurt you if I can help it."

"Promise?"

Robert took his index finger and crossed his heart. "Hope to die."

Mona snuggled closer to Robert on the couch. "We'll be happy, won't we?"

"No one will touch us," Robert promised.

Little did Robert know when he uttered those words that he would be proven wrong.

Trouble was fast approaching.

Other Books By Abigail Keam

Mona Moon Mysteries

Princess Maura Tales

Josiah Reynolds Mysteries

Last Chance For Love Series

About The Author

Abigail Keam is an award-winning and Amazon best-selling author. She is a beekeeper, loves chocolate, and lives on a cliff overlooking the Kentucky River. She writes the award-winning *Josiah Reynolds Mysteries*, *The Princess Maura Tales* (fantasy) and the *Last Chance For Love Series* (sweet romance).

Don't forget to leave a review! Thank you. Tell your friends about Mona.

Join my mailing list at: www.abigailkeam.com

You can also reach me at Instagram, Facebook, Twitter, Goodreads, YouTube, and Pinterest.

Thank you again, gentle reader, for your reviews and your word of mouth, which are so important to any book. I hope to meet you again between the pages.